The Phantom of Faerie Mountain

E M McIntyre

The Phantom of Faerie Mountain

Book 1: The Red King Trilogy

United States of America

ISBN-13: 978-0-9988993-0-5

ISBN-10: 0-9988993-0-5

To my family for their love and support.
Without you, my dream would have stayed just that...
And to my dear mother,
though I finish this journey without you,
you are forever infused
throughout the pages of my imagination.
May we meet again someday.

Book 1

The Red King Trilogy

1

*M*oisture clung to the windshield as an eerie blanket of fog enveloped the car, forcing Abby's sister to bring the vehicle to a crawl. Abby stared into the murky night, releasing a long sigh. *We'll never get back to the cottage at this rate.* "Why did Dad have to take such a late train? He knows you don't like driving home through the Highlands at night," Abby groaned.

"Quit complaining, Abby. You're just upset because he's always traveling up north. You know his obsession with old books; nothing will keep him from adding to his collection." Sage pulled the car to the side of the road. "We'll have to stop here for a while. I can't see anything through this fog; we don't want to run into any stray sheep."

Abby flipped the radio on and scanned the few stations that tuned in. Talk radio, bagpipes, and something dreary. Abby turned the radio off and resumed staring into the fog. Sage began one of her usual, annoying rants about how Abby should quit acting so depressed. "Just because we aren't in the States anymore doesn't mean your life is over. Wait and see. You'll make new friends once you start school again." Sage winked. "Who knows, maybe you'll even meet a cute Scottish lad."

Blah, blah, blah, she's worse than Dad. Abby zoned out her sister's sermon and concentrated on the fog. The thick soup swirled around the lights from the car, allowing no entry or escape. A ghostly feeling washed over Abby. She eyed her sister, wondering if Sage felt uneasy as well. Sage continued rambling on about how great life would be in Kinloch-Rannoch, oblivious to the form materializing from the fog.

Suddenly, every hair on Abby's body stood on end. Something green, glowing, and shaggy stepped into the path of the headlights. It walked on four legs like a dog, but it was the size of a tiger. Its unkempt fur looked like wiry wool. Powerful muscles propelled its smooth stride toward the driver's side door.

Abby looked frantically to her sister. "Sage." No response. "Sage!" *What's the matter with her! This isn't happening, this isn't happening!* Abby shook Sage's shoulders, realizing her sister seemed to be in a trance. In desperation, Abby pounded on the horn. At that moment, the creature locked eyes with Abby as if it hadn't yet noticed her.

Abby drew a deep breath. *Close your eyes. If you can't see it, it can't see you. Yeah, right, who am I kidding? I'm not five.* Abby froze in her seat, following the creature's movements with her eyes. *What is it? It looks like a giant wolfhound on steroids or something, but I've never heard of a green dog, let alone one with glowing, green ooze all over it!*

The beast rounded the car, stopping inches from Abby's door, hot breath snorting from its nostrils, condensing on the window. Bit by bit, Abby turned her head toward the window and willed the quivering of her lip to stop. The creature let out a low, menacing growl. Abby whimpered, "Pl, please don't hurt us."

As if in reply, a calm, tingling sensation wrapped itself around Abby's mind. It was like something, or someone, was inside her head, searching her thoughts for something unknown. *Uh...*

A gruff, deliberate voice entered her mind: *The Red King must set me free.*

"Wha, what?" Abby choked in a whisper. The beast blinked, entering her mind once again. *The Red King must set me free.*

Abby sat transfixed, hypnotized by the creature's piercing gaze. She wanted to scream or cry or close her eyes, but she couldn't look away. After a few moments, the creature raised its head, turned with a snort, and strode back toward the road. Disappearing into the thick fog, it paused for one purposeful glance back at Abby.

The Red King must set me free.

Then it was gone.

Abby stared in disbelief out the window. *Did that really just happen?*

***

Sage flicked her eyes, turned to her sister, and scrunched her face in surprise. "Abby, why in the world are you so pale? And why are your hands trembling?"

Abby clasped her hands together and looked in the rear view mirror. Shocked by the loss of color in her face, it took Abby a moment to understand just how scared she must have been. Abby mumbled, "Well, I, uh...well, you'd be pasty white too if that thing had been inches from your face!"

Sage frowned. "Abby, what on earth are you talking about?"

Abby snorted, "Uh, the giant, grimy, green dog-thing that came out of the fog like a phantom. Are you saying you did not see that?"

"Abby, your mind must be playing tricks on you. There was no green 'dog-thing.'"

"Yes there was! It said something about the Red King freeing him."

"It talked to you?" Sage paused and rolled her eyes. "Abby, dogs don't talk."

"Well, it didn't exactly talk. It was more like it was inside my head."

"Abby, I don't understand where all this is coming from, but there was no dog."

"But..."

"Abby, when we get to the cottage why don't you take a long, hot bath and clear your mind."

"There's nothing to clear. I know what I saw!"

"Abby, end–of–discussion. I don't want to hear about it again."

Abby crossed her arms, "If Mom were alive, she'd believe me."

"Abby, look at me." Sage paused, softening her voice. "Mom would probably have told you to take a hot bath too." Abby stared into the clearing fog, pretending not to feel her sister's touch on her shoulder.

"Abby, I don't know what's going on with you tonight,

but I know you really miss your friends in Nebraska and our old house." Sage sighed and fingered the gem nestled in the curve of her throat. "Listen, Abby," she continued, "I'm certain if Mom would have had the chance to know you, she'd want you to have this."

Brushing aside the sole blond ringlet amidst her chestnut curls, Sage disconnected the clasp of her necklace. "I've been thinking about this for a long time and intended to give it to you in September for your birthday, but I think you should have it now."

Abby glanced suspiciously at her sister. "Why would you want to give up your amulet?"

"When Mom first gave me this, she said it would banish my bad dreams forever." Sage flashed a playful smile at Abby. "Maybe it will take care of your phantom, monster-dog."

Abby began to protest but thought better of it. Feeling the smooth cut of golden crystal, she placed the treasured ornament around her neck. "Thanks Sage, I promise to take good care of it." Abby leaned back in her seat, sighing softly. The mysterious fog had rolled out, revealing the star-filled night.

Shifting into drive, Sage drove toward their cottage. Abby stared out the window as the still, dark waters of Loch Rannoch flowed by. Trying to reassure herself she wasn't crazy, she replayed the scene over and over in her head. She knew what she had seen.

Sage may not believe me, but I bet old Mrs. MacTavish will!

2

A hot bath and restful night's sleep did nothing to clear Abby's head. Visions of the phantom dog raced through her mind as she pulled the cottage door tight behind her. Shivering in the cool morning air, Abby zipped her hoodie snug and hurried across the street to her father's book store. Cookie-cutter buildings with speckled gray bricks lined the road, brought to life only by splashes of color from late-spring flowers planted along the row. As Abby entered the store, a familiar, musty odor teased her nostrils.

"Guid morning, Lass." A squat, pear-shaped woman popped up from behind the counter.

"Good morning, Mrs. MacTavish," Abby replied, as if speaking to a teacher.

The woman squinted at Abby over her wire-rimmed glasses, placing one gnarled hand on an ample hip. "What brings ye across the way so early in the morning?"

Abby looked down, tapping the toe of her hiking boot against the base of an ancient bookshelf. "Oh, I thought I'd do a little research in my dad's books. That's all, nothing special."

"Research, eh?" Mrs. MacTavish continued to peer at Abby over the top of her glasses. "Anything I can help ye with?"

Abby hesitated. *I don't want old MacTavish thinking I'm crazy too, but she might be able to help me.* "Well, um, have you ever heard of some type of strange dog that roams the area around here, maybe something magical?"

Mrs. MacTavish lifted a grayed eyebrow. "Magical dog ye say? Aye, I have, but why is a young lass interested in such a thing?"

Abby controlled her eagerness to find answers, "Oh, it was just something I heard about. I thought it would be fun to learn more."

The old shopkeeper motioned for Abby to follow. "I imagine yer father has a book back here somewhere that will tell ye something."

Wooden bookcases lined the walls of the narrow shop from floor to ceiling. Abby couldn't imagine how her father could find room for even one more book. *Surely there must be something here.* Mrs. MacTavish stroked her chin as she scanned the uppermost row of the last bookcase. "Now let me see, perhaps one of these will do the trick." Pulling a wobbly step ladder over to the shelf, she started to climb.

"Uh, Mrs. MacTavish, would you like me to get the book down?" Abby suggested, envisioning the old woman crumpled on the floor, buried under a pile of books.

"Nonsense! I may be old, but I'm not helpless!" Mrs. MacTavish scrambled to the top of the ladder. "Aye, here we are: *Scottish Myths and Folklore.* Why don't ye start with this, Lass, and see what ye find." Passing the yellowed book to Abby, the old woman descended safely to the floor.

Abby seated herself at the only table in the shop. "Thank you, Mrs. MacTavish."

"Ye're welcome, Lass." Mrs. MacTavish again peered at Abby over the top of her glasses. "Ye've had no breakfast yet?"

"No, ma'am."

"Well then, I'll bring ye a spot of tea and some fresh baked shortbread." With a mischievous twinkle in her eye she added, "Or perhaps I could interest ye in some haggis?"

Abby crinkled her nose in disgust at the thought of sheep guts. "Shortbread would be perfect, thank you."

Smiling inwardly at the old woman, Abby opened the book's thick, ornate cover. She looked at the copyright page. *Wow. Eighteen eighty-eight, but it looks like this book's never been touched.* Abby gingerly parted the crisp pages, flipping through them one by one. She stopped at the first illustration. A cat, black as night, stared into the outside world from the slick page. A caption was printed under the picture in bold, scripted letters.

> Cait Sith. A monstrous fairy cat that many Highlanders believed to be a transformed witch. Wayward travelers feared crossing paths with this wicked beast and its razor-sharp claws.

Yikes, I'll stick with my monster-dog, thank you! Abby continued scanning the pages.

> Grey Dog of Meoble. A gigantic, shaggy-haired, Scottish deerhound. The grey dog was said to appear to those of the MacDonald Clan who were nearing their time of death.

Abby sighed. *Well, my dog was green, and we're*

Fletchers, not MacDonalds, so that couldn't be it.

Feeling discouraged, Abby neared the end of the book. Turning the next page, three words jumped out at her.

The Red King.

Abby's heart raced as she read on.

> A brave and honored Scotsman of the late 12th century who protected Highlanders from the Sidhe.

Abby traced a complex symbol upon the page with her finger tip. *Hmmm. This is the 21st century, it couldn't possibly be the Red King my dog was referring to, could it? How could someone from the 1100s free him? That doesn't make any sense.*

And what on earth are the Sidhe?

***

As if reading Abby's mind, Mrs. MacTavish appeared holding a silver tray loaded with shortbread and a pot of tea. "Here ye are, dearie. Is there anything else ye need?"

Abby pointed to the book. "Well, how do you say this word and what's it mean?"

Mrs. MacTavish leaned over Abby's shoulder. "Aye, ye pronounce that as 'shee.' The Sidhe were said to be feisty faerie people of the Highlands. Mischievous little buggers if you ask me." Catching herself, she added, "According to old stories, that is. Now is there anything else ye need before I get back to inventory?"

Abby shrugged. "Are there any other books to look at? There was nothing like what I saw last night in this one." Abby paused, horrified, realizing what she had said. "I mean, nothing looked like what I heard about."

Mrs. MacTavish froze momentarily, but pretended not to notice. "Aye, I think there may be one other book in the store room." The shopkeeper disappeared through a darkened doorway, returning moments later. "Perhaps this will have yer answer," she said, placing a thin, glossy, green book in front of Abby. "Be gentle with this one, it belonged to yer mother."

Abby's eyes widened. "This was my mom's? Why was it in the storeroom?"

"I imagine yer father wanted to keep it safe."

"Safe?"

"It was yer mother's favorite, Lass. She always had her nose in that book, before we lost her."

Abby looked the old shopkeeper square in the eye. "What happened to my mom, Mrs. MacTavish? Dad never wants to talk about it."

Mrs. MacTavish stared into space for a moment before replying. "Oh, it was a terrible, terrible day, Lass. Yer mother always enjoyed exploring new places, she did."

The old woman squeezed Abby's hand. "A sheepherder saw yer mother that night near the Well of Fair Maidens, just before a dreadful storm rolled in. Authorities say she must have been knocked into the empty well by a gust of wind, slipping into a connecting cave shaft far below. The storm washed so much debris into the shaft; it was sealed off from the outside world." Dabbing one eye with the hem of her apron, she continued softly. "The poor dear was never found."

Abby fingered her amulet, struggling to hold back tears. "I don't even remember her."

"Ye were just a babe, Lass. Thirteen years ago it was; Sage was only six. Yer father was so distraught; he took ye girls back to his grandfather's farm in the States."

Abby stared at the cover of her mother's book. *Peoples of Faerie Mountain.* Wiping her eyes, she asked, "Where's Faerie Mountain?"

"Practically right under yer nose, Lass." Mrs. MacTavish squeezed Abby's hand again. "Step outside and ye'll see it to the south, just a stone's throw away."

"But that's Caledonia. Faeries supposedly lived there?"

"Aye, Lass, but don't get any thoughts in yer head about going there. Yer father would throw a fit if he knew I'd let ye see that book."

Abby smiled. "I appreciate you showing it to me, really. And for telling me about my mom."

Nodding, Mrs. MacTavish drew herself up to her full five feet and spoke in a business-like tone. "Well, sit and read as long as ye'd like and let me know if ye have any other questions. Yer old enough to start thinking for yerself now, Lass."

As the old woman bustled off to continue her work, Abby stared at the book's cover, imagining her mother studying the same illustration years ago. Green-skinned men and women danced among the trees at the base of an ominous mountain. Abby gently flipped through the pages, absorbing every line of text, her mind returning to the mystery at hand.

> The faeries were fond of beautiful humans, often stealing them away.

She snorted softly. *I wonder what they would want with humans?*

It was rumored the faeries employed a magical dog, the Cu Sith, to seek out and kidnap young maidens for a fate unknown. The Cu Sith was said to roam the hills of the faerie mountain and surrounding areas. Many accounts report the Cu Sith as terrifying and black as its counterpart, the Cait Sith.

An enormous, jet-black dog filled the page. Abby thought back to the previous night. *Well, it's the right size, but the wrong color. So that's not it, either.*

She turned the page and gasped. A giant, shaggy, green dog gazed back at her. Abby's heart pounded as visions of her encounter flooded her mind. She read on.

However, other accounts describe the faerie dog as glowing green, with shaggy fur and a braided tail.

This is it! That's my phantom! Abby could barely contain herself. *But what was he doing here? And now? And why weren't Sage and I 'kidnapped for a fate unknown'? And why did my mom have a book like this?*

Tucking a stray curl behind her ear, Abby took a deep breath. *OK, it's not even noon yet, I bet I could bike to the footpath going up to Caledonia, search around, and be back before dark. Sage will never miss me. Maybe I can find some clues about this Cu Sith. It will drive me crazy if I don't look!*

Abby closed her mother's book, placed it on the table, and quietly slipped out the door. *I'll grab my backpack and a few supplies, and then I'm off to Caledonia!*

3

A bby coasted to a stop in a barren parking lot, then dismounted her bike and flipped the kick-stand in one fluid motion. *This sure beats exploring the flat prairies back in Nebraska. Not that this is much of a mountain, but it should be a good climb once I get through the woods.*

Remnants of a forgotten forest stretched across the countryside to the base of the mountain. The forest floor, covered with a thick layer of pine needles, felt spongy under Abby's feet. Birds flitted from branch to branch and an occasional squirrel scurried up a tree as she approached. The terrain gradually sloped upwards as Abby picked her path through the trees.

Why do I feel like someone is watching me? Abby paused, scanning her surroundings. *Hmm. Weird. Wonder if they have Sasquatch in Scotland?*

Laughing at herself, Abby continued to the edge of the forest and out onto the open hillside of Caledonia. Boulders great and small speckled the landscape as if tossed haphazardly by a giant. As Abby neared the largest boulder, she noticed something was odd about it. *That one actually looks like a giant!* The enormous stone resembled a misshapen man, hunched low to the ground. A worn stone marker stood next to the boulder. A familiar symbol accompanied words that caused Abby's heart to flutter as she read them out loud.

"Here we lost our protector: The Red King."

Abby contemplated the marker. *If this is supposed to mean that the Red King is dead, how can he free my phantom? I must be on the right track though, but where to now?* Abby turned in a circle, surveying the hills around her. *If I were a huge, green dog that glowed like a neon sign, where would I go when I wasn't out kidnapping fair maidens? It gets cold and windy on the mountainside. Maybe I might hide in a cave . . .*

Spotting what looked like a rocky path, Abby made her way up the north slope, taking care with the placement of her feet. The wind whipped her hair, and she pulled her hoodie snug over her head, tightening the draw strings. *I wonder if Mom ever explored here.*

Halfway up the slope, Abby lost her footing and slipped several feet, a handful of grass bringing her to a stop. After regaining her step, she spied an unusual outcropping some twenty feet to her right, with a narrow opening that looked like a cave entrance. Abby swung her backpack to the ground. *Well I'm sure it's going to be dark in there; I'll need my flashlight.* After a few moments of rummaging, Abby retrieved the light, shouldered her pack, and approached the opening with caution. "Hello, anybody in there?" After an eternity of silence, Abby shined the light through the opening and entered the cave.

Smooth walls, a broad shoulder length apart, twisted and turned endlessly. After what Abby estimated as thirty feet, the cave walls opened up into a large chamber. Abby paused at the opening. "Hello, monster-dog." She breathed softly and was certain moments later the only sound she heard was that of her own heart beating.

Abby scanned the walls, ceiling, and floor with her light. The chamber extended for a generous twenty feet, with no other exits. Nothing seemed unusual to Abby, but she guardedly followed her light to a spot in the back of the cave where the wall indented several feet. *No dog back here. No nothing back here.* As Abby turned to exit the chamber, something in the indention of the wall caught her attention. *Is that a carving?* Abby brushed a layer of dirt off the wall with her hand, revealing a symbol she now knew by heart. *The Red King.* Abby stepped forward to examine the wall further and stumbled over a rise in the floor, the full weight of her hand pressing on the carving.

Startled, Abby stepped back as a soft grating sound echoed throughout the chamber. She focused her light on and around the carving. A small cubby hole opened up next to the symbol. *There's something in there! It looks like . . . a hot dog without the bun!* She hesitated, unsure about touching her discovery. *What if I reach in and it's booby-trapped?* After a moment, Abby relaxed, composed herself, and reached into the hole, wrapping her fingers around something leathery.

Abby clamped her teeth on the end of the flashlight to free her hands and carefully examined her find. It was a roll of leather, wrapped with a thin braid of rope that was tied in a simple knot. Abby worked the knot, freeing what looked like a scroll. *This sure is soft even though it's probably been in here a long time.* Abby unrolled the leather to find a strange writing inside. *This might be*

Gaelic, but I'm not sure. Maybe if I show it to Mrs. MacTavish she'll know what it says. I bet it's something important. Why else would someone hide it in here? Anxious to get back to the bookstore, Abby rolled up the scroll and tucked it in her backpack.

Swinging her pack into place, Abby focused her light on the cave floor as she turned toward the front of the chamber. An eerie green glow illuminated the exit tunnel. Abby slowed her pace as goose bumps covered every inch of her body. *Oh no, I know that glow. I don't think I'm alone anymore!*

***

The Cu Sith entered the chamber with slow, determined steps. Abby inched her way backwards into the depths of the cave. The creature stopped a tail-length away. Abby gulped, deciding this was no phantom. With her back flat to the cave wall, she considered her options. The only exit was behind the beast and she was sure she couldn't outrun it; it could clamp onto any body part with little effort if it desired. Abby froze as she felt the unusual tingling in her head. *The Red King must set me free.*

Without thinking, Abby blurted, "But the Red King is dead!"

The voice in her head was insistent. *No, Lass. He lives.*

"But that marker on the hillside and the book..." Abby paused, realizing what had just happened. "Hey! Wait a minute! You can understand me?"

The dog seemed to nod, stepping closer. *Place your hand upon my head.*

Abby pressed her body firmly against the wall. "Are you crazy? You could bite my hand off!" Her head tingled again as she fought to control her shaking knees.

Trust me, Lass.

"I can't," she answered in a whisper.

You can. Trust me. Trust yourself.

Abby hesitated, unsure, drawing back as far as she could. The dog leaned in further, its hot breath washing over her face. Abby stared into its eyes. She felt like bees were buzzing in her brain. *Now, Lass.*

Transfixed, Abby slowly raised her hand past the beast's formidable canines. A warmth washed over her as the creature entered her mind one last time. *He must set me free.*

Abby squeezed her eyes shut, inhaled sharply, and with a burst of courage, flopped her hand onto the creature's head. To her surprise, it didn't feel slimy at all- it felt soft and safe. Without warning, Abby was knocked into a whirlwind of blackness. She felt as if she were falling and spinning and standing firmly all at the same time, while engulfed in a world devoid of light. She tried to scream but found no voice. Abby thought the wild sensation would never end. But then, it did.

4

*A*bby felt herself drop to the ground. Her back ached and for a moment, she was blinded by daylight as she cracked her eyes open. While trying to orient herself, she realized her back hurt because she had landed on something hard, lumpy, and scratchy. She grunted, trying to sit up, but her arms and legs seemed to be tangled.

Feeling herself propel forward, she heard an unfamiliar voice cry out, "Get aff me! Ye broke me bowe!"

Abby rolled onto her stomach and craned her neck to find the source of the racket. A lean, muscular, young man brushed debris from what looked like a woolen tunic and leggings. Fiery red braids hung low to his chest. He scowled, examining his cracked bow. "Numpty!"

"Numpty?" Abby jumped to her feet, scooping up her backpack. "What's that supposed to mean?"

The young man glared at Abby, "Numpty, stupit lad!"

With her hands on her hips, Abby snorted, "I am not stupid! You're the one that was in the way when I fell." She narrowed her eyes at him. "And I'm no lad!" Abby unzipped her jacket and pulled the hood back, revealing wild chestnut curls with a ringlet of yellow falling across her eye. "Who are you, anyway?"

The young man gazed at Abby, mesmerized. Abby waved her hands in front of his face. "Hellooooo, who are you? What's your name?" She pointed to herself. "I'm Abby Fletcher."

As if awakening from a dream, the young man replied, "I'm Rory MacKay, Lass. But why do ye don the clothes of a lad?"

Abby rolled her eyes, "I am not dressed like a boy; lots of girls wear jeans and hiking boots and hoodies. Besides, why do you have piggy-tails?"

With a blank look, Rory repeated, "Pig-gy-taels?"

Abby demonstrated by tugging on invisible braids at her neck. The young man, in turn, gave his braid a puzzled tug, cocking his head at Abby. "I don't know what a pig-gy is, but this is no tael, Lass."

"And what's with the tunic and the bow?" she continued. "Are you going to a Renaissance Faire?"

Rory sputtered, shaking his head. "Yer speakin' a strange language, Lass. What are ye doin' on the mountain? I've niver seen ye here."

Abby contemplated the question and pointed over her shoulder, "I was exploring that cave back there when I must have tripped and I, well..." Abby redirected Rory's question, uncertain of what had just happened. "What are you doing on the mountain?"

Rory gestured at his broken bow. "Was huntin' a deer 'til ye frightened it. Was me denner for a week!" Rory surveyed the woods with a nervous look in his eyes. "Look, it's gettin' dark. Won't be safe for ye out here. We need to go."

Abby gave Rory a suspicious once-over. "You may be

cute, but I don't know you. I'm not going anywhere with you!"

"Lass, be serious. Ye should know there's nestie fowk in the woods. It won't be safe for us."

Picking up on Rory's accent, Abby considered his point. *I've never heard anything about 'nasty folk' in the forest, but then again, I never expected a green monster-dog to talk to me either!* Thinking back to her encounter in the cave, Abby turned to look up the hill. "I can't leave yet," she replied. "I have to find my dog."

Rory gripped his bow. "If yer dog has any sense, it's already made its way through the woods!"

Abby hesitated, deciding it would be better not to mention the dog was a green, glowing beast that could enter her mind and talk to her without speaking. "Well, okay, I guess it will be dark soon and I should get home, so I suppose we can walk together if you want."

"Aye, Lass, now yer bein' smart. This way." Rory took Abby's arm and started off toward the woods, guiding her along a trail.

After several minutes of making their way down the mountainside in silence, Abby noticed something seemed off with her surroundings. She stopped to scan the tree line again - her jaw dropped. *What the heck...there's ten times as many trees ahead as there were earlier. What on earth is going on?*

Rory grabbed Abby's hand and pulled her forward. "Let's go, Lass! It's almost dark." As the duo weaved through the scattered boulders near the bottom of the mountainside, Abby stopped again, this time in front of her 'giant' rock. "Hey! Where'd the marker go?"

Rory looked back at his bewildering companion, waving his bow in the air. "Marker? What do ye mean?"

"What do you mean, 'What do I mean?' The stone marker that was next to this giant boulder that looks like a man?"

Rory frowned, "I've niver seen a marker." His frown turned to confusion as he paused. "What's a marker?"

Abby leaned against the boulder as a momentary dizziness washed over her. Rory's clothing, his bow, his rough accent, the trees, the missing marker - Abby refused to believe the possibility. "Rory, I have an important question for you, and please don't look at me like I'm crazy . . .What year is it?"

Rory rolled his eyes and looked at her like she was crazy. "What year?

Abby grew frantic. "Yes, what year? Or better yet, who's your king?"

"Don't be daft, Lass. Everyone knows Robert the Bruce just claimed the crown!"

***

Robert the Bruce? Abby slumped to the ground, her legs turning to wet noodles. *Robert the Bruce...Robert the Bruce.* Abby gasped, recalling scenes from one of her favorite movies. *Oh geez! If Robert the Bruce is King, then that means I'm in the early 1300's. Sage really won't believe this one, if I ever see her again!*

Rory trudged to Abby's side and hoisted her by the armpit. "There's no time to be restin', Lass."

Abby squirmed from Rory's grip, stamping her foot

with a huff. "I need to gather my thoughts. Mister monster-dog just dropped me seven hundred years from my home and I have no idea how to get back. So I don't care if there's 'nestie fowk' in the woods!"

Rory stepped back to examine his companion. "Have ye gone mad, Lass? What is a monster-dog? An' what are these words ye speak of? Seven hundred years?" Rory eyed the band on Abby's wrist. "An' what," he questioned, motioning with his bow, "is that?"

Abby sighed with impatience. "It's my watch. You know, for telling time."

Rory crossed his arms, grunted, and raised a suspicious eyebrow. "An amulet that tells the passin' of the sun? No such thing. Are ye a witch?"

Abby's jaw dropped in disbelief. "Don't be silly! Witches don't exist. And besides, if I were a witch, I already would have turned you into a rat for being so annoying!"

"Yer fortunate me mither an' faither taught me different than most fowk around here." Rory's nostrils flared as a robust hooting emanated from the darkened forest. "Look, witch or no witch, it's no' safe here. Eyes are upon us. We must be aff."

Abby considered the situation and pushed herself to her feet. "Alright, I'll go with you, but quit calling me a witch!"

Taking Abby by the elbow, Rory guided her through the trees, quickly at first, then slowing to a stop every few feet to listen. This was not the same forest Abby had traversed hours before. Blackness threatened to envelope them, save for the occasional sliver of moonlight breaking through the canopy.

Rory paused in a shaft of light, looking back at Abby and holding a finger to his lips. As they stood frozen in silence, Abby heard the sharp crack of a branch behind them. Rory silently produced a small dirk from a sheath at his waist. Abby felt her stomach rise. *Oh great, a knife. Just what exactly does he think is out there?*

Before Abby could react, grimy arms wrapped themselves around her from behind, while a huge man with wild hair jumped from the trees and knocked Rory to the ground. Abby yelped in surprise. "Rory!"

"What 'av we 'ere?" A low, raspy voice breathed in Abby's ear. A man in rags spun her to face him, twisting her backpack to her side.

"Let go of me you greasy pig!" Abby attempted to kick her assailant but slipped on the spongy forest undergrowth. She was saved from falling by the man's painful grip on her left arm. Pulling Abby close, the man chuckled as he flicked the lone, golden ringlet of her hair with the tip of a short sword. "Well, well, Masters Mavis and Tavis will fatten our purse for this one."

Abby glanced toward Rory and saw he had righted himself, slashing at his opponent with his dirk. Squirming in her captor's grip, Abby clutched her backpack with her free arm, wishing for a weapon of her own. After a hasty mental inventory of her belongings, she slipped her hand in her bag and fumbled around.

"What ye got in 'ere, Lassie?" The man's breath smelled like old socks. He chuckled again. "Whatever ye 'ave, it's all mine now!"

Abby pulled her hand out of her bag, producing a

container of pepper spray her father insisted she carry with her. "You better let go of me, Slimeball, or you'll regret it!" Abby pointed the can at the man, aiming straight for his beady eyes.

The man loosened his grip on Abby's arm and stared quizzically at the strange item in her hand. Tightening his hold again, he exclaimed, "Oh, no, Lassie. Yer goin' to see me masters."

"Don't say I didn't warn you!" Abby pressed the can's trigger with her thumb, turning her head as a stream of spray shot into the man's eyes.

The man let out a deafening roar, releasing Abby's arm. "Ayyeeee! Me eyes. I can't see. What evil is this? Ye witch!"

As the man rubbed his eyes in desperation, Abby stamped on his foot with her hiking boot for good measure, sending him into a renewed uproar. Regaining focus as her attacker stumbled into the darkness, Abby turned to find Rory.

"Aye, ye see, he thinks yer a witch, too!" Rory leaned forward, hands on his knees, his assailant nowhere to be seen. Catching his breath, Rory frowned upon his now un-reparable bow and tossed it to the ground.

"Very funny." Abby scowled at Rory but was relieved to see him unharmed. Replacing the can of pepper spray into her bag, Abby straightened her hoodie, wiped her hands on her jeans, and strode forward. "Let's get out of this forest. Now!"

5

*A*bby sat quietly on a grassy knoll, gazing at the vast, star-filled sky. The full moon cast a comforting glow, revealing rolling hills and deep valleys that stretched as far as she could see. Rory sat at Abby's side, humming a tune she didn't recognize.

Rory glanced at Abby. "What troubles ye, Lass? We're safe now, out of the forest."

Releasing a long sigh, Abby surveyed the landscape, knowing there would be no parking lot, no bicycle, no way back to Sage, her father, or Mrs. MacTavish. "I don't know. This is all pretty confusing."

Rory placed a gentle hand on Abby's shoulder. "Lass, let's keep goin'. It's no' far now."

Abby hesitated, trying to make sense of their encounter in the forest. "That creepy little man said something about taking me to his masters. I think he called them Mavis and Tavis. Do you know what he was talking about?"

Rory laughed at the names. "That thief has gone mad if ye ask me. There's been talk in the hills of nestie faerie fowk, twin brothers to be exact, using foul magic on unsuspectin' travelers." Pausing, Rory took Abby's hand

and squeezed it softly. "But I've niver seen a 'faerie' on these lands, or his supposed masters. In fact, I don't believe they exist. It's all rubbish."

Abby shrugged. "Well, I suppose you'd know better than me. But if I see those slimeballs again, I'm not sticking around to find out!"

Rory smirked. "Ye needn't worry. Yer witchy powers will make them think twice."

"Ha ha, Numpty!" Abby rose to her feet. "Which way now? I'm cold and hungry, so let's get to it."

Rising, Rory motioned westward toward Loch Rannoch. "By the black waters, beyond the nearest hill."

As they walked, Abby thought about their strange situation. Half joking, she declared, "I hope your parents don't get weird about you showing up late at night with a girl."

Rory halted and stared beyond Abby with no response, a hardened look on his face.

"Did I say something wrong, Rory? What's the matter?"

"I buried me faither not long ago and me mither died when I was just a lad."

Abby blushed and wished the night sky would cover the embarrassment so evident in her cheeks. "Oh. Sorry. I didn't mean to upset you. My mother died when I was just a baby, so I kinda know how you feel."

"It matters not, Lass." Rory looked into Abby's eyes. "I'm sorry ye lost yer mither." With a mischievous smile, he added, "It's no wonder ye wear the clothes of a lad!"

Abby swatted at Rory's shoulder, stifling a laugh, "You're hilarious, Numpty. Let's get moving."

The duo crested the nearest hill. An enormous lake lay at the bottom, a good ten minute walk by Abby's estimation. An orange glow danced to the north of the black waters. Rory froze, absorbing what lay in front of him. Abby poked her companion in the side. "Hey, what's the problem? Do you think those pigs from the forest are making a campfire?"

Rory broke into a sprint down the hillside. "No. It's me hame!"

***

Abby stood puzzled. "Your hame? Your home?" Abby followed as fast as she could, taking care not to tumble down the hill. By the time she reached the bottom, she was certain her lungs were going to explode. Abby stopped to catch her breath but Rory continued like a madman toward his house, some hundred yards away.

Abby could see now Rory's small home was completely engulfed in flames. In the distance, she could hear him belting out words that were foreign to her, but clearly full of rage. Abby ran toward the inferno, stopping to assess the situation once she reached the fire. Rory was headed to the lake with a small bucket. Staying back from the flames, Abby raced around the tiny house frantically looking for anything else she could use to carry water. She wanted to scream. *Where's a fire hydrant and hose when you need one!* Rory rushed back to the house and tossed the water from his bucket onto the flames. To his dismay, the fire took no offense to his assault as it consumed the water. Rory turned toward the lake again, but Abby grabbed his arm and spun him around. "Rory, there's nothing you can do."

"No, Lass, yer wrong. I must get more water." Rory pulled away from Abby's grasp and ran for more water, only to see the flames swallow it up once again.

"Rory, I'm sorry. It's just too late."

"No!" Rory hesitated but seemed to accept the hopelessness of his efforts. With a groan, he dropped the bucket and slumped to the ground, pulling his knees tight to his chest. "It's all I had left of me mither and faither. Me faither's books, the ones he used to teach me to read. And his sword. And me mither's things - the apron she always wore when tendin' our denner, and a kerchief embroidered with a red rose that still carried her scent. It wasn't much, but it was all I had."

Abby sat next to him and put her arm around his shoulder. "I don't know what to say Rory. This is horrible. Maybe in the morning, when the fire has stopped, we can search the remains to see if anything is salvageable."

Rory stood and turned away. Shadows from the fire flickered on his cheek. "Me faither once said his sword was as precious as his life. I should no' have left it behind while huntin'."

Abby frowned. "Well, wasn't it made of metal?"

"Aye. It was forged of the finest metal by me faither's ancestors."

"Well, then, certainly it will survive the fire." Abby rose and moved toward Rory, gently laying her hand on his arm. "We'll find your father's sword in the morning, once the flames have burned out. I'm sure of it. But now I think we'd better try to sleep some. I'm exhausted and I'm sure you must be too."

Rory turned to Abby with a look of resignation. "Yer right, Lass. There's nothin' to be done tonight." Gesturing to a level patch of ground not far from the fire, he continued. "Ye rest here, where the fire will warm ye. I'll keep watch for a bit."

Abby knew it would be pointless to argue with him, so she stretched out and mashed her backpack into the least uncomfortable position she could find and laid her head upon it. Rory sat next to her and began to hum a sadder version of the same tune he'd hummed on the knoll, and before she knew it, Abby drifted off to sleep.

***

Abby shivered and cracked a weary eye, shielding her face from the bright morning sun. Her stomach grumbled and she felt the need to take care of personal business. She sat up and groaned, rubbing the side of her neck and shoulder, reminding herself never to sleep on a backpack again. Then she caught sight of the charred remains of Rory's home and her heart sank.

"Good morn, Lass." Rory sat slumped forward, gazing at the ashes.

Abby reached over and touched his back. "I'm so sorry, Rory. Did you sleep any?"

"Aye. A bit." Rory brushed his cheek, sat up straight, and turned toward her. His eyes looked red. "I've been waitin' for ye to wake. Are ye hungered?"

Abby's stomach reminded her the last food she consumed was Mrs. MacTavish's shortbread. She snorted,

"Hungry enough to eat a horse!"

Rory looked at her with surprise. "A horse? No, ye should niver eat so grand a beast." He paused as Abby stifled a laugh. "I can trap a kinnen if ye like."

"Kinnen? What exactly is that?"

Rory lifted a single finger to either side of his head and twitched his nose.

"A rabbit!" Abby envisioned, with great horror, the process of catching, cleaning, cooking, and eating one of her favorite childhood pets. "Um, no. Thanks though. I think I have something in my bag to eat." Abby unzipped her backpack and dug to the bottom, producing a peanut butter granola bar. Opening a smaller side pouch, she pulled out a mini water bottle. "Here, I'll share with you."

Rory stared with wonder and suspicion. "What is that?"

"This is a bottle for carrying drinking water. It's made from plastic."

"Pla-stick?"

Abby giggled. "Never mind, maybe I'll explain it later." She opened her snack bar and broke it into two pieces, holding out a section for Rory.

Rory hesitantly took the food, sniffed it, and shrugged, biting off a chunk. Abby sensed it was all Rory could do not to spit his mouthful to the ground. She uncapped the water bottle and held it out to him. "Here, take a sip of water. It will help with the stickiness of the peanut butter. And do not spill the bottle, it's all I have!"

Rory accepted the water and washed down the food, then handed it back to Abby along with the rest of the granola bar. "I'll trap akinnen after I find me faither's sword."

Abby shrugged, finishing the rest of her bar. "Suit yourself. Don't blame me though when you're hungry later and can't catch a rabbit."

Rory rose and surveyed the remnants of his home. A few embers continued to cast a red glow in the dim morning light, but most of the fire had run its course. He stood silent for a moment then looked over his shoulder, his eyes full of sadness. With a soft voice he said, "The ashes have cooled enough to look for me faither's sword. A-by, would ye help me please?"

It took a moment for Abby to realize this was the first time Rory had called her by name and she much liked the way it sounded. She jumped up and brushed herself off. "Of course I will! But could you give me just a minute? I need to, um, I need to go to the bathroom first." Rory stared at her. Abby shifted her weight from leg to leg and blurted out, "I need to pee!"

Rory snorted. "Aye, that." He pointed to a nearby knoll. "Ye may do what ye need on the other side, if ye like."

Abby nodded appreciatively. "I'll be right back! But be careful if you start without me – the sword still might be hot." Abby scurried over the tiny hill and completed her mission with relief. All the while, she could hear Rory rummaging through the debris. Then she heard desperate yelling.

"It's gone! A-by, It's gone!"

Abby hurried over the slope and back to the house. "What do you mean it's gone?"

"Me faither's sword! It's gone!" Rory pointed to a spot

that had once been the back wall of the house. "The sword was kept in this corner. It's no longer here."

Abby waded into the ashes, which came well above her ankles in places. "Well, maybe the sword got knocked away in the fire or was moved by falling debris." She kicked at an unusually large pile of ash, which exploded in a cloud of tiny gray particles that stuck in her throat upon inhaling. Stifling a cough, Abby moved toward Rory. "Let's keep looking."

As Rory turned to reply, his face suddenly went pale. In one swift movement, he pulled his dirk from its sheath and motioned with his free hand for Abby to move behind him. Abby's stomach lurched as she glanced over her shoulder to see what Rory was looking at. Not ten feet away stood a giant, green dog.

6

Rage flushed through Abby's face. She whipped around and stomped toward the dog. Rory stretched forward and caught Abby by the arm, pulling her back toward him. "What are ye doin', A-by? The beast is sure to harm ye!"

Abby wriggled from Rory's grip and pushed his armed hand toward the ground. "Rory, relax. This is my dog I was telling you about. I need to, um, talk to him."

Rory raised an eyebrow. "So now ye can talk to animals? Well, I'd say either yer mad or ye really are a witch!"

"Trust me for a minute, Rory. You can tease me later all you want, but this is real. If I'm going to have any chance of getting home, I need to talk to him." Abby paused with the most genuine look she could muster. "Ok?"

Rory groaned and relaxed, then sheathed his dirk. "Aye, but if the beast hurts ye, it's goin' to be me denner."

Feeling satisfied Rory wouldn't start a fight, Abby turned and marched toward the creature, stopping inches from its nose. She narrowed her eyes and spoke under her breath, flapping her arms for emphasis. "You've got some nerve!" she growled. "You said I could trust you and look at what you've done! I almost broke my back, had to fight off a mugger in the forest, and now our only form of shelter has burned to the ground!"

The animal tilted its head and almost seemed to smile. Infuriated, Abby stomped her foot and added, "I demand you take me home right now!"

Suddenly, Abby's head tingled as a low, amused rumble came from the creature. *Are you finished, Lass?*

"I will be when you take me home!"

The dog shook its head. *I cannot do that.*

Abby crossed her arms. "And why not?"

You must find the Red King. He must release me.

"And I'm supposed to do that how? I'm a fourteen-year-old girl you just plopped into the 14th century all by herself." Abby looked to Rory as he paced nearby, suspiciously eyeing the dog. "Well, with the exception of him."

Ask the boy to help you.

Abby frowned. "I don't know about that. His house just burned down and his father's sword is missing. Rory has enough problems of his own. I wouldn't feel right asking him."

Rory stopped in his tracks when he heard his name. "Ask me what? What are ye and this creature talkin' about? And why can't I hear it?"

Abby pulled at her hair with frustration. "I don't know why you can't hear him! I hear him in my head and he understands me whether I talk out loud or just think the words."

"What? Well, that's daft, Lass. Prove it to me."

Abby tried not to sound annoyed. "Prove it to you?

And how do you propose I do that?" She rubbed her temples and thought for a moment. "Okay, what if I ask him to tell me something about you I would have no way of knowing?"

Rory looked at the dog, then at Abby. Finally, he nodded, with a glint in his eye. "Very well, Lass. Ask it me faither's name."

Abby rolled her eyes. "And how exactly is he supposed to know your..."

The dog's voice cut into Abby's mind. *Alistair MacKay.*

Abby stopped mid-sentence. "Oh. Okay. He says Alistair MacKay."

Rory stood silent in disbelief. "How could ye know that?" He said, shooting a puzzled glance at the dog. After a moment, he looked to Abby. "How could he know that?"

Abby shrugged. "I don't know how he knows. But now do you believe he can talk to me?"

Rory grunted. "No. Was a lucky guess." He kicked at a stone, then looked up again. "Where was me mither born?"

Abby felt an amused voice in her head. *In a small burgh near Inverness.* She turned to Rory. "He says in a small burgh near Inverness."

Rory let out a yelp and pulled at his braids. "No, this can't be." He spun around and glared at the dog, striking a challenging pose. "Well, ye can't possibly know me mither's given name!"

Abby held her breath, waiting for a response from the animal. Hearing no immediate answer, Rory pointed in triumph. "Hah! It doesn't know!"

Then the answer tingled in her head, and Abby

repeated it softly. "MacKenzie."

"Ach!" Rory threw his hands up, and began dancing about as if possessed. "This can't be! I don't believe it!" After a moment he stopped and eyed the animal. "So, assuming I do believe it can talk to ye – with some kind of witchy power . . ." He paused and sighed. "What is it called? And what does it want?"

Abby shrugged again. "Well, ah, I don't know, I never thought of him having a name." She turned her attention to the dog. "So, what is it? Do you have a name?"

The familiar tingle washed through her head. *My name is Finlay.*

Abby looked to Rory. "He said his name is Finlay."

Rory snorted after a moment of contemplation. "That means 'white warrior.' I think yer dog is confused. There's nothin' white about him."

Abby rolled her eyes in response. "And your point, Numpty?"

Rory shrugged. "What does the creature want?"

"He says I have to find the Red King."

Rory shook his head. "No, there's no such thing, a fancy tale the Red King is."

"Well, according to a book I just read, he was killed a couple hundred years ago by faeries causing problems in this area."

Rory rolled his eyes. "I don't have time for this. I must find me faither's sword. Are ye goin' to help me or no'?"

The dog nudged Abby's arm with its nose. *You must find the Red King. Make a deal with the boy.*

Abby thought to herself, *Okay, Okay. I'll see if he'll help me find the Red King if I help him locate his sword. I don't know why you just don't go find him yourself!*

It would mean my death.

Abby raised an eyebrow at the beast. *Your death? I don't understand any of this...*

In time, Lass, in time.

Abby sighed, refocusing on Rory. "All right, I will help you find your sword but you have to promise to help me find this Red King. Ok?"

Rory moved toward the remains of his home and started poking at the debris with his foot. He paused to look Abby in the eye and grunted. "Aye, I give ye me word. I wish I knew where to start though, A-by. I don't think the sword is here."

Finlay entered Abby's mind again. *Tell him to cross the lake.*

Puzzled, Abby repeated the message. "Finlay says we should cross the lake."

Rory looked as though he had been struck by lightning. He jerked his head around as his face turned a burning shade of red. "I should've known," he exclaimed. "The Robertsons!"

***

"The Robertsons? Who are they?"

Rory continued to fume. "They're two brothers who've been sneakin' around here since me faither passed."

"So you think they stole the sword? Well let's go steal it back from those jerks then!" Abby paused, turning back to the dog. "Hey, Finlay, why do you think the Robertsons took it?" She did a double-take when she found she was talking to herself. Abby groaned. "Figures he'd disappear like that."

Rory headed toward the lake. "Ye should stay here, A-by. Will be dangerous."

Abby ran after him. "No way! We made a deal. I'll help you get your sword and you help me find the Red King. Period. Besides, I'll probably be safer with you even if there's a bunch of thugs across the lake."

Rory scowled but nodded in agreement. "We'll use me boat. Will be faster than walkin'."

Abby followed Rory to the lake shore, shivering as a light wind created ripples in the water. Gray clouds crept across the sky. *I hope it doesn't rain. That's the last thing we need right now.*

Rory pulled a small boat from its hiding spot in the long grasses near the shore. The boat looked like it had been carved from a tree trunk. Abby wondered about its construction and hoped it would withstand the long journey across the lake. She estimated the opposite shoreline was at least a mile away.

Rory pushed the boat into the water and motioned for Abby to get in. "Have a seat, A-by." Recognizing the uncertainty in Abby's eyes, he added, "Don't worry, it's safe...I made it me-self."

Without much confidence, Abby placed a hand on Rory's shoulder for balance and carefully stepped into the boat, trying not to rock it. There was no bench to sit on, but the interior was smooth. She sat down on the bottom of the boat and put her backpack between her legs. Rory pushed off from shore and clambered into the vessel, oar in hand. With strong, rhythmic motions, stroking first on one side of the boat, then the other, he propelled them into open water. Abby frowned as the sky darkened and the winds picked up. "I think it's going to storm."

"Don't worry, A-by." Rory pointed across the waters to the southwest. "There's a hut on that island me faither used during long fishing days. We'll shelter there if the winds come hard. But a little rain will no' harm us."

Abby shrugged, trying to hide her uncertainty as the motion of the boat jostled her stomach in every direction possible. The pair remained quiet for nearly a quarter-hour as Rory concentrated on moving the craft efficiently. Abby watched the veins in Rory's forearms pulse and wriggle with his efforts as a lone droplet of rain hit her cheek. She looked to the sky and then to the increasing waves and moaned.

"We'll stop at the island, A-by. Don't be afraid. We'll be there soon."

Abby clenched the sides of the boat. "I'm not afraid," she said stubbornly, "I'm just not a fan of swimming in open waters during a storm!"

Seeing the worry in Abby's eyes, Rory changed the subject to distract her. "A-by, tell me about yer family, yer hame."

Abby sat quietly for a moment, surprised by the question. "Well, my father collects books and is always traveling around the country looking for 'hidden treasure' as he calls it. He just inherited his grandfather's book store in Kinloch-Rannoch, so he moved my older sister, Sage, and me here a couple months ago."

Rory questioned further with a wink. "And what of yer sister, A-by. Is she a witch too?"

Abby snorted. "Okay, first of all Rory, there is no such thing as a witch, not the kind you're referring to at any rate. And second, no making fun of Sage. She may be boring, but she is my sister...and she has pretty much taken care of me my whole life."

Rory stopped rowing momentarily, putting his hands up to signal defeat. "Sorry. Where is Kinloch-Rannoch?"

"Oh, well, ah, if you'd believe it, it's in the same area your house is...ah, was, but it won't be established for a long, long time."

Rory shook his head and resumed rowing with long, deep strokes. "I don't understand. Ye say yer seven hundred years from yer hame. How did ye get here? How can such a thing be? It's difficult to believe."

Abby shrugged. "I don't know how it's possible, just that it is. I am as confused as you are, Rory." She lowered her eyes and added softly, "I don't blame you one bit for not believing it. All I know is Finlay came to me near my home, twice, and the second time he told me to touch his head. As soon as I touched him, he zapped me here and dropped me on top of you. And now I'm supposed to find the Red King and he won't take me home until I do!" Abby took in a deep breath. "I'm afraid I'll never see my family again."

Rory rested the oar across his knees, leaned forward, and placed a strong hand on Abby's shoulder, looking into her eyes. "A-by, ye have me word I will see ye hame. Ye will be with yer family again." With determination, he swung the oar back into the water and continued paddling toward the island.

Pretending to be reassured, Abby turned her attention

to the increasing rain drops. Suddenly, a flash of lightning ripped across the sky, followed almost immediately by a clap of thunder. Abby could feel the tingle of the electricity in the air. "Wow! That was close. Hurry, Rory!"

Rory rowed with increased fervor as Abby turned to see how far they were from the little island. To her relief, they were but twenty yards from a rocky shore.

As they approached the shoreline, the waves seemed to double in strength. Sheets of rain exploded from the sky and a huge wave lifted them upwards. Abby cried out as the boat seemed to go airborne. They came down with such force Abby thought she must have been split in two. She looked between her feet and realized the boat was fractured and taking on water at an alarming rate. The wave had thrown them onto the rocks by the shoreline, puncturing the boat's hull.

Rory leaped from the boat onto the rocks, yelling something Abby couldn't hear over the howling wind. He gestured wildly, holding out a hand to her. She grabbed his hand and quickly shouldered her bag. Rory pulled her out of the boat, and they scrambled over the rocks to solid land just as the vessel released from its fate and began to sink. The pair stood helplessly on the shore, shivering, as they watched the boat disappear into the lake. Rory placed his mouth close to Abby's ear so she could hear him. "I'm sorry, A-by," he shouted. "The boat is gone. I'm afraid we're stuck here."

7

"Stuck?" Abby yelled. "Can't you do something?" She strained to hear herself over the wind.

"What?" Rory gestured he couldn't understand her and grabbed Abby's hand, pulling her across the shore into a band of trees. As they headed toward the center of the island, the wind abated and the trees offered some protection from the rain. Still, Abby felt cold and tired and wished only to be home in the comfort of her father's bookstore. Pushing their way through the forest, the two reached a small, squarely-constructed hut that sat in an opening among the tall pines. Rory motioned Abby inside.

Moist pine needles covered the floor of the hut, with a small ring of rocks in the center that Abby assumed was a fire pit. A squat tree stump served as a seat, and a small knapsack rested in the corner. Feeling rain on her face, Abby looked up to see a roof thatched with old pine branches now bare of needles. The rain was coming down more heavily in the clearing, easily finding its way through the failing roof. Rory worked methodically outside, pulling the old branches from the roof and hacking off fresh boughs from the nearest tree with his dirk to fill in the holes. When the roof was solid once again, Rory entered the hut, dripping from head to toe.

"Thanks, Rory." Abby could smell the scent of the newly-cut pine boughs wafting through the hut. "That was pretty impressive. Well, except for the boat sinking, of course." She plunked herself down on the stump and began to wring water from her hair as Rory stomped and shook himself dry. Abby sighed heavily with exhaustion. "So, now what?"

Rory shrugged. "We wait for the storm to pass. Then I'll see if I can build a raft."

A raft? Abby managed a weak smile, wondering how Rory would build a raft and how long it would take. With a long, slow exhale, she leaned forward to avoid the occasional drop of rain that squeezed through the roof.

Noticing Abby was shivering, Rory walked over to the knapsack and pulled a long, woolen blanket from the bag. He moved toward the entrance of the hut to shake the dust from the blanket. Rory then wrapped it around Abby's shoulders. "This should warm ye, A-by."

Abby blushed at Rory's kindness. "Thanks. You need a blanket too though; you're soaked to the bone!"

Rory waved his hand to the side, dismissing the thought. "It's alright A-by, I'm no' cold." Rory overturned the pine needles on the floor of the hut with his foot, revealing a dry layer beneath. He sat down on the dry needles next to the tree stump and pulled his legs close to his chest. Abby could see the gooseflesh on his arms.

Abby stood up from the stump and copied Rory's actions on the hut floor. She plopped down next to him and spread the blanket across them both. "You look pretty chilled, Rory, so we can share the blanket." Rory grunted but did not argue the gesture.

The pair huddled together in silence for some time, listening to the howling wind and the occasional crack of lightening. Abby soon became aware of her closeness to Rory beneath the scratchy blanket. Feeling a wave of awkwardness, she broke the silence, hoping for a distraction from Rory's intermittent shivering. "So, you've been all alone for a while now, huh?"

Rory shrugged, staring through the open doorway into the forest. "Aye."

"Do you mind me asking what happened to your parents?"

Rory smiled as if remembering something special, but sadness soon filled his eyes. "Me mither and faither lived far to the north, on the lands of Clan MacKay. The laird of the castle, Ian MacKay, was a 'greedy, barbaric monster', so me mither said. He was always fightin' with the neighborin' clans and would send his strongest men to raid villages." Rory shivered again, and Abby sensed it wasn't from the cold.

"Those barbarians would steal cattle and do whatever awful things they could get away with. Me faither didn't agree with the doings of Ian MacKay and would try his best to avoid the raids." Rory stared at the ground and continued so softly Abby had to strain to hear. "Me faither was a peaceful man, a woodworker and scholar. He didn't take to fighting."

Rory paused in thought. After a moment, Abby interjected, encouragingly, "Sounds like your parents weren't happy pledging allegiance to this 'Ian'."

Rory nodded. "Aye. They didn't want to have anything to do with his ways."

"Were you born yet?"

"No. I was inside me mither when they decided to flee the MacKay lands."

"How were they able to get away? It must have been dangerous!"

Rory laughed softly. "Me faither loved to tell me about the night me mither saved him from 'evilness'. As the story went, Ian MacKay was planning to raid the land of the Sutherland's. But this was no raid like the others. MacKay had his eyes set on claiming that land for his own, so he ordered his men to leave no survivors...to burn everything to the ground."

Rory's voice rose as he continued. "Me faither refused to take part and tried to slip away from the raiding party. But a guard followed him hame and burst in, demanding me faither join the others, lest he be drawn and quartered for insolent behavior."

Abby drew a sharp breath. "Gosh, what did your father do then? You said he was a peaceful man. He probably didn't know much about fighting, huh?"

With a glint in his eye, Rory slipped from the blanket, hopped up, and pulled a small pot from the knapsack. "It was me mither who reacted with force." Rory waved the pot above his head. "When the guard pulled his sword, me mither snuck up behind him and knocked him on the head with a pot." Rory imitated his mother's actions, swinging the pot down onto an imaginary head. "'Be gone with ye!' she cried." Rory dropped the pot, and pointed to the floor of the hut. "And the guard fell flat to the ground with no sense about him." Rory staggered about. He flopped down flat on his back in front of Abby, trying to look senseless. When Abby giggled, he opened one eye and propped himself up on an elbow. "It didn't take me mither and faither long to gather up their few belongings and escape into the night atop the guard's horse."

"Wow. And so they came here then?" Abby cocked her head. "But doesn't your land belong to someone else? How were they able to stay there?"

"Aye. Me faither built our hame on the Robertson's land, who had good dealings with many of the clans Ian MacKay raided. Alan Robertson accepted me faither's promise of loyalty in exchange for our safety on his land."

Rory rose and began brushing pine needles from the back of his tunic. Moving to the stump, he drew his dirk, and began to whittle a small pine branch while he talked. "Me faither agreed to fish and do woodworking jobs for Robertson, and in turn, Robertson promised me family would be left alone."

Abby nodded, trying to imagine what it would be like to start life over in a strange place where she didn't know anyone. Then she realized, with a start, she would have to do exactly that, right here, if she couldn't get back to her own home in her own century.

Again painfully conscious of her predicament, Abby pulled the mini water bottle from her pack and found only a few drops remained. She looked up at Rory, who had fallen silent while concentrating on his whittling. "Rory, I hate to interrupt whatever you're making there, but I'm pretty thirsty. I think we need to figure out how to get some water."

Seeing the empty bottle, Rory dropped the branch, sheathed his dirk, and jumped to his feet. He grabbed the pot from the floor and bowed to Abby. "As ye wish, yer witchy-ness!" With a wink, Rory stepped outside the hut. Moments later he returned, the pot full of water.

"Where'd you get that?" Abby exclaimed.

Rory brought the pot to Abby. "Me faither built a catch basin behind the hut."

Abby eyed the water suspiciously. "That's wonderful Rory, but I think we need to boil this before we can drink it!"

Rory lifted the pot to his nose, sniffed the water, and pulled his head away quickly. "Awf. Ye're right, A-by. I'll have to show ye how to start a fire then, won't I!"

***

Rory entered the hut with an armful of small, dead pine branches and motioned for Abby to join him at the fire pit. "Ye see, even though it's rainin', ye can find dry limbs close to the base of the trees." Rory began snapping the sticks into small pieces and scooped several handfuls of dry needles into the center of the pit. He arranged the sticks over the needles into the shape of a teepee. "Now we need a flint to start the fire." Rory searched the knapsack, shaking it upside down when he didn't find what he was looking for. He stood and scoured the corner of the hut and groaned. "No flint."

A flip switched in Abby's head as she unwrapped herself from the blanket and grabbed her backpack. "I might have some matches, or even a lighter ...I like to be prepared for anything, you know." Rory looked at Abby blankly and she remembered he wouldn't know about matches or lighters. *Great, he really will think I'm a witch now!*

Abby rummaged to the bottom of her bag, wrapping her fingers around a small cardboard box. "Bingo!" She pulled out a small box of matches. Rory continued to stare at her quizzically. "Okay, Rory, you aren't going to understand this, but this is pretty common where I'm from, so don't get all weird on me." Rory relaxed his shoulders and attempted a comical face.

Abby smiled and pulled out a match. "These are matches," she instructed, "and you use them to start fires. It's the same idea as a flint. You strike the stick against the side of the box here where it's rough. See?" she said, holding the box out for Rory to examine. "The rough edge ignites a flame on the stick...there's nothing witchy about it."

Abby struck the match and it caught fire immediately, producing a warm glow on her face. Rory jumped back as the flame ignited, then moved closer, staring with wide, curious eyes. Abby carefully lowered the match into the rock ring and lit the dry pine needles, which sparked with fury. After several moments, the small sticks started to burn. Feeling pleased, Abby sat and warmed her hands over their creation. "Now we need to boil the water."

Rory nodded and grabbed the knapsack, wrapping it around the handle of the pot to protect his hands. Then he crouched and held the pot over the fire.

After a quiet minute, Abby spoke. "So, what happened after your parents moved here, if you don't mind telling me?" she asked. "Things seemed to be working out for them."

Rory stared into the fire, silent for several moments. "One day when I was a wee lad, me mither was cookin' a pot of stew and complained her head hurt. Me faither approached her and she fell limp in his arms, dropping the stew to the ground. There was nothin' to be done. She was gone."

Abby gasped. "That's so sad, Rory. I'm really sorry. You must miss her immensely."

"Aye. I long to feel the warmth of her arms around me again, and to hear her singin' to me, but it was her time. She didn't suffer on her passage."

The pair was quiet again for several minutes, contemplating the losses in their lives, the crackle of the fire filling the void. "So what happened to your father then, Rory, if it's not too hard to say?"

Rory sighed heavily, removing the boiling water from the fire to cool. "No' long ago, me faither went into the forest to gather wood. He didn't come hame, so the next day I went to find him. I searched all day, and when the sun was almost past, I came upon him. He lay quiet on the forest floor. He was cold and didn't move when I shook him."

Abby spoke in a hushed voice. "Again, I'm so, so sorry Rory. Do you know what happened to him?"

Anger filled Rory's eyes. "Aye, I do. He was murdered!"

8

"*M*urdered?" Abby jumped up and shrieked in dismay.

Rory slumped by the fire. "Aye. Ran him through with a sword. He was defenseless."

"Well do you know who did it?"

"I've heard talk a MacKay was sent to hunt him down in payment for his disloyalty to the clan."

Abby paced to the doorway and back. "But why would it take them so many years to find your father? And why didn't they come after you, too?"

Rory stood and shrugged, then stared into the fire again. "I don't think they expected to find me family on rivaling land or that they knew me mither was with child when they fled." He looked at Abby and sighed, frustration filling his eyes. "I don't imagine his killer knew of our hame. He must have come across me faither in the forest by chance, otherwise I don't think I'd be sittin' here with ye now."

Abby moved to Rory and placed her hand on his arm, looking him square in the eye. "I'm glad they didn't know about you Rory. And I'm so sorry. I can't even imagine how you must feel." Abby dropped her hand and backed away, thinking about her mother's death and wondering how she would feel if someone had murdered her father. "You must have been so angry," she decided. "Didn't you want to just hunt down the murderer and run him through, too?"

Rory contemplated the question before answering in a calm voice. "Aye. I've countless visions of doin' to that 'pig', as ye would say, what he did to me faither. But no, me faither would look upon me with sad eyes for such actions. He didn't rear me to act in that way, and I will no' disappoint him in death."

Abby nodded slowly, feeling it was time to change the subject. Chilled by Rory's story, she sat down by the fire again. "Well, so what about your father's sword? Why is it so special? And why would the Robertsons want to steal it? You were really angry when Finlay suggested they took it."

Rory snorted. "Alan Robertson's sons, Duncan and Banner, were instructed to set camp across the lake to keep watch on me family...to make sure we kept our end of the bargain and to see no one brought trouble to us." He shook his head. "I don't know why, but those Robertson brothers didn't seem to care for us. For many years they honored the agreement, but since me faither passed I've seen them sneakin' round our side of the lake, drinkin' spirits and actin' peculiar. Would be no surprise if they stole from me."

Abby jumped to her feet with a renewed energy. "Okay then! We have to figure out how to get off this island right now and spy on those lunk-heads. If they have your father's sword, we will get it back!"

Rory bent down to test the temperature of the water in

the pot, then gestured for Abby to hand him her bottle. "Will be no easy task gettin' off this island A-by. I've only me dirk...will take many hours to cut through branches sturdy enough to construct a raft. And it's too wet to climb trees for the proper branches right now." He shrugged an apology. "We'll have to wait."

Frustrated, Abby passed her water bottle to Rory, who carefully filled it from the little pot. "Well, okay," she conceded. "It just feels like nothing is going right." Rory grinned and handed Abby the full bottle. "At least we've got drinkin' water!"

Rory sipped from the water remaining in the pot, passing it to Abby once he had his fill. "Drink the rest of this water," he directed. Then he motioned toward her bottle. "Save the pla-stick for later."

Abby raised the pot to her lips. As she did, a warm, green glow began to seep into the shelter, and this time Abby couldn't be happier to see it. She swallowed the water from the pot in one gulp and exclaimed, "Finlay!"

***

Abby hopped up and dashed to the formidable shape now filling the entry to the hut. Without thinking, she leaned in and wrapped her arms around the dog's neck, soaking up the warmth emitted from his thick coat. Though it was still raining, the creature seemed soft and dry.

Finlay sniffed Abby's clothing. She could feel him speaking in her head. *You are frozen through, young one. This will not do.*

Abby laughed weakly, straightening herself and motioning toward the ring of rocks. "Tell me about it! Luckily, we got a fire started. I think my clothes are starting to dry a little."

Finlay eyed the inside of the shelter and continued to talk in her head. *You must get dry. Come with me to the back of the dwelling and lie on one side of me, with the boy on my other side, then place the blanket over all three of us.* Seeing Abby's skeptical look, Finlay continued. *Tell the boy not to argue and not to pull his weapon.*

Abby shot a glance at Rory, who was pacing around the hut, hand on his dirk. Considering the warmth of Finlay's fur, Abby turned to Rory with an air of authority.

"Rory, Finlay is going to help us warm up and dry out. I know you aren't going to like this much, but it's for our own good. He's going to lie down in the back of the hut and he wants us to lie on either side of him, then I'll put the blanket over us."

Rory squinted and moaned. "I don't trust him, A-by."

Abby rolled her eyes. "It will be fine, Rory. I don't know why, but I have a strong sense he means no harm. In fact, I think he's meant to protect us."

Rory nodded reluctantly. "If ye trust the creature A-by, it's good enough for me."

With that, Finlay gracefully moved to the back of the shelter. Rory stepped to the side as Finlay stretched himself out to an impressive length on the pine floor. Abby lay on the ground in front of the dog and scooted her back up against his belly. Rory hesitantly laid down on the creature's other side, turning his back to the animal but sliding in close enough to feel its warmth. When both were settled, Abby tossed the blanket over them and snuggled tightly against Finlay.

Concentrating in her head, Abby thought, *I can't believe how warm you are. And why is it you look like you just stepped out of a vat of green jello, yet you are soft and dry? That's pretty bizarre you know.*

Finlay gently bumped her cheek with his snout and replied. *You are quite the curious one, Lass. That will get you into trouble if you aren't careful.*

Abby snorted. *Well, I don't see how I can get into more trouble than I'm already in! I'm lost in time and stuck on this little island, and I'm talking to a green, gooey-looking, gigantic dog...in my head no less!* Abby paused, deciding to push the subject. *So, tell me. Why do you look so strange?*

Finlay lay silent for several moments, then entered Abby's mind again, speaking soft and smooth. *The answer to your question will lead you down a dangerous path...one you may not reverse and one that may have terrible consequences. I regret I have already placed you in the situation, but it was the only way. Are you prepared to face such challenges?*

Abby let her body soak up Finlay's warmth as she considered his words. *Well, I imagine I don't have a choice, do I, seeing as how you say you can't take me home. So, lay it on me fuzz-ball. Why are you green?*

Finlay puffed a hot blast of air at Abby's face. *You must learn to show respect when appropriate, Lass. You don't want the fuzz-ball to make a snack of you, do you?* Finlay smacked his lips in a mock munching sound.

Abby tensed momentarily, but realized Finlay was teasing her. Still, she was reminded of the animal's tremendous power and made a mental note to treat him with more consideration in the future. *I'm sorry, I didn't mean to be disrespectful,* she thought with sincerity. *But could you get on with it already?*

***

Finlay enveloped Abby's mind as never before. Flashes of imagery danced throughout her head, forcing her to clamp her eyes shut as he began to speak.

Ages ago, faeries ruled the grand mountainside of Caledonia and thrived on disrupting the lives of innocent common folk. Finlay spoke in low, rich tones. *After decades of turmoil, a protector emerged from the countryside wielding a great magic capable of combating the faeries. He would be known as the Red King for his flaming braids and majestic stance.*

Oh, geez, not the Red King again, Abby thought, before remembering Finlay could hear her.

The creature continued, ignoring her mental outburst. *No one knew where he came from, but it was rumored the last of the great Magicians, Sylvan Myst, summoned him from another realm to protect his beloved land and kin. For many years, the Red King protected the Highlands until one day a grave battle ensued.*

Images of the Red King overwhelmed Abby's consciousness. *It is said a force of faeries ambushed the Red King and slew him upon a giant rock. However, his remains were never found.*

Confused, Abby blurted out, "Well I don't understand what that has to do with you or me!"

At the sound of Abby's voice, Rory leaped to his feet, dirk drawn. "What is it, A-by? Are ye all right?"

"Geez, I'm sorry Rory." Abby felt like she was losing track of when she was thinking and when she was talking out loud. She rolled onto her back and looked up at Rory. "I didn't mean to wake you. I was just talking to Finlay. Please try to go back to sleep."

Rory stared back at her for a moment. "Hmpf," he noted and laid down again, back-to-back with the giant dog, pulling the blanket over him.

Abby rolled onto her side and adjusted the blanket. *Okay,* she thought to Finlay, making sure she wasn't actually talking. *So what does all of this have to do with me?*

Finlay's voice rumbled in her head. *Patience, child, and it will become clear to you.*

Abby relaxed and opened her mind. Finlay's rich voice began to enchant her once more. *The last act of Sylvan Myst was to cast a spell banishing the faeries deep inside Caledonia, trapping them for eternity where they could do no more harm.*

Abby imagined hordes of wicked little faeries imprisoned inside a mountain, chipping at the stone with pick axes and spitting chewing tobacco on each other. *So did it work?*

Somewhat. Almost all of the faeries were banished. Even though Sylvan's spell was powerful, two of the worst managed to escape punishment. And those two have schemed and contrived since that day to find the key that will release their kind from banishment.

Abby imagined how dreadful it would be for all the vile

faeries to be released. And what was the deal with the two escapees? And how did it involve her? She turned her thoughts back to Finlay. *So, I suppose you're going to tell me these escaped faeries are somehow making you do something for them?*

Aye, Lass. Do not underestimate them. Finlay paused, searching for the right words. *I was unfortunate to have crossed paths with the pair while searching a cave one day. They sensed my 'specialness' and bound me with their magic.*

Gears started turning in Abby's head. *Hmm. I saw this book that depicted faeries as having green skin. Is that why you are green...because they bound you with their magic?!*

Finlay snorted in affirmation. *That is so. As long as their spell envelops me, I am forced to do their bidding and return to the heart of their dwelling in the mountain.*

So how are you able to be here with us then?

My 'Masters' believe I am out hunting.

Masters? Abby craned her neck toward Finlay. *Wait a minute! Finlay, what are their names?*

Mavis and Tavis.

Abby went stiff as she recalled her encounter in the woods. *Those rotten thieves wanted to take me to them! Finlay, do you know what the faeries would want with me?*

Finlay lay in silence for some time. *I have said enough for the time, Lass. Right now you must focus on finding the Red King. He must free me.*

But...

Finlay snorted softly. *No, young one, warm yourself and go to sleep. You must wake when the stars shine bright.*

Exhausted from the day's events, Abby yawned at the thought of sleep and craned her neck to look into the dog's eyes. *Why then?*

Finlay appeared to smile. *Because that's when I'm getting you off this island!*

9

A cool breeze brushed against Abby's cheek, followed by a warm nose. A soft, yet hurried voice called to her at the outskirts of her mind. *Rise young one, you are dry and rested. The time is now.*

Abby cracked her eyes to find Finlay standing over her, the blanket partially hanging from his back. The dying embers in the fire ring, combined with the green radiance from Finlay, cast an eerie glow through the darkness. Abby stretched her aching body. "Why so urgent?" she questioned with a yawn.

The sky is black now. You need the cover of night. Finlay swung his head to examine the sleeping form of Rory. *Wake the boy now, Lass. I'm surprised he can sleep through his own snoring.*

Abby giggled and sat up. She called Rory's name, gently shaking his shoulder. When Abby received no response, she wiggled Rory's shoulder with vigor and called his name with force. "Rory. Time to wake up!"

Rory shot to his feet, drew his dirk, and squatted into a fighting stance. "What?" He asked with great concern, squinting through the green glow. "What is it? Did the beast hurt ye?"

Abby rolled her eyes. "No, Numpty. Finlay didn't hurt

me."

Rory relaxed, sheathed his dirk and straightened himself with a hint of irritation evident in his face. "Then why are ye waking me again, A-by?!"

"Well, for your information, Mister Crabby-Pants, Finlay says he's going to get us off this island. He says we need the cover of night, but for what, I don't know."

Rory grunted. "Right. And just how is an overgrown dog going to get us off this island?"

Abby stifled a nervous laugh. "Well, ah, we hadn't exactly discussed that yet." Abby turned to Finlay. "Well, you heard him. How exactly do you plan to get us off this island?"

Finlay approached Abby, touching noses with her. *I will remove you from this island the same way I brought you to where you are.*

Abby stepped back and stamped her foot. "Oh no you won't. I nearly broke my back the last time!"

Finlay let out a low growl, causing Rory to draw his dirk again. *You have no choice, Lass. Either you accept what I offer or remain here for who knows how long. Consider your decision carefully.*

Abby thought quietly for a moment, motioning to Rory to stand down. She knew Finlay was right, but was unsure how to explain what they were about to do. She looked at Rory. "Ok, so it's like this. Obviously you understand Finlay is 'special', right?"

Rory sheathed his dirk, crossed his arms, and stared at Abby without responding.

"Okay then. Well, I don't know how it is possible, but Finlay has the ability to move himself around places, like teleportation I guess."

Rory tightened his arms and continued his blank stare.

"Okay, I guess you wouldn't know what that means. Um, well, think of it as one minute you are in one spot, like in this hut, and the next minute you are wherever you want to be, like in the forest. You cross the distance without actually having to travel there. You just zap yourself where you want to go!"

Rory rolled his eyes and scoffed. "Right."

Frustrated, Abby moaned. "Look, I know it's confusing and unbelievable, but I experienced it myself! That's how Finlay brought me here. I don't understand it either, but it's real, and it's our best chance of getting off this island! Unless you have any better ideas?"

Rory sighed and dropped his arms to his sides. "I told ye I'd build a raft, A-by."

"That will take days, Rory, and besides, we don't have any food!"

Finlay stepped in between the pair. *Enough, little one. Grab the boy's hand and touch my head. It will be over before he knows it.*

Abby protested in her mind. *But...I don't want to deceive him! He has the right to choose, he shouldn't be forced!*

Finlay's chest rumbled with impatience. *Take his hand now, Lass. He will understand your choice in time.*

Abby hesitantly rounded Finlay, grabbed her pack, and took Rory's hand. "I'm sorry Rory, but we need to do this. Everything will be fine in a minute, you'll see." Before Rory could react, Abby looked to Finlay, nodded, and placed her hand on his soft head. The room flashed a brilliant green, then everything went black.

***

This time, Abby felt an odd weightlessness and a cold wind pushing past her. She wasn't sure, but she had the impression of being whisked across the lake, inches above the water. In seconds, she tumbled to the ground, landing amongst scratchy thistle. She righted herself in the darkness and did a quick pat-down to check that she was still in one piece. "Well, I guess we have the dark of night, all right," she observed.

Rory groaned several feet away, but stood as quickly as Abby did. "A-by, don't do that again!" he whispered, unsure of their whereabouts.

Abby gingerly cleared the distance between them, peeling a thistle from her hoodie. She apologized in a low voice. "Rory, I'm really sorry. I didn't want to trick you, but we needed to get out of there. And look, we're in one piece, although I have no idea where we are."

The pair stood silently for a moment, trying to get their bearings. Suddenly, a strong gust of wind rustled through the tall grasses, carrying the faint sound of voices. Abby jerked her head toward the sound and started to speak, but Rory motioned for her to remain still. The source of the voices seemed distant, but Abby was certain two men were arguing; over what though, she couldn't tell.

"It's the Robertsons," Rory stated with conviction.

Abby strained her ears. "Are you sure? What are they

saying?"

Rory shrugged. "I don't know, but we're goin' to find out!"

The duo traversed the shoreline silently, toward the sound of the voices. Rory motioned for Abby to follow him into a lone stand of pine trees as they neared the area where the men were arguing. With only partial moonlight to guide them, they moved cautiously from tree to tree until they were some ten feet from stepping into an open clearing.

A stone's throw away stood a small, dilapidated house. The roof needed tending and a gaping hole was visible along the back of the structure. Light from a roaring fire flickered beyond the structure, casting long shadows of the two men who were now engaged in an intense shouting match. One man, short and lean, shook a walking stick at the other while tending to food on a spit over the fire. The second man, no taller, but with a scraggly beard and a huge belly, drank from a cup and belched loudly.

The lean man poked his stick at the other's bulging belly. "Banner, if ye don't make haste, ye won't get to the castle before sun-up. Yer sure to get a lashin' this time. Faither has grown tired of yer insolence."

The man with the drinking cup sat heavily on a log and waved a dismissive hand in the air. "Ye should go this time, Duncan. I shall stay here to tend the fire and guard the ale." He belched again, his head bobbing toward his chest.

Still hidden in the shadows, Abby poked Rory and whispered, "It is them, Rory. It's Duncan and Banner

Robertson!" Rory nodded and moved closer, stopping just short of the clearing. He crouched down and listened intently.

"I'm no' playin' around this time, Banner," the thin man sputtered. "Faither said fer ye to report. Take the horse and go. Now!"

Head still bobbing, Banner Robertson belched and dropped his cup to the ground. With his chin on his chest, he began to snore loudly. Seeming to lose all patience, his brother raised his walking stick and brought it down on Banner's ample belly with a squooshy whack. From her hiding place, Abby thought the noise sounded like someone striking a giant marshmallow, and she had to cover her mouth to stifle a laugh.

Stunned by the blow, Banner jumped up with a start, swaying back and forth before the fire. "Ye needn't thrash me Duncan," he whined.

Duncan Robertson continued to hold his walking stick aloft, as though to deliver another blow. "Needn't I? Ye'd sleep the night if I didn't...then we'd both get a thrashin'."

"Well, ye don't have to be so grouchy." Banner rubbed the growing welt on his belly and began to stagger to the horse. "Ye think yer so smart, just cuz yer older!" Gathering the reins, Banner made a pathetic effort to hoist his bulk onto the horse's back. After several failed attempts, he gave his brother a pitiful look. "Could ye give me a hand?"

Duncan crossed to the horse and boosted his bulbous brother with a grunt, nearly tossing him over the other side of the animal. Grabbing the horse's mane, the heavy man teetered precariously on top for a few seconds, but managed to steady himself. "There. That wasn't so bad, eh Brother?"

As the horse started off slowly, almost without guidance, Banner shifted his impressive girth and motioned for Duncan to bring him his skin of ale. "No, ye've had enough, Banner," came the gruff reply. "Let the ride clear yer head."

"Me head is perfectly clear!" Banner declared with a glazed expression. "I'll be back in a fortnight with supplies." Belching loudly a final time, he directed the horse into the darkness, calling out into the night. "Don't drink all me ale while I'm gone."

Still hiding in the shadows, Abby rolled her eyes, wondering how these two had survived together for so long. She could see Rory shaking his head in amazement.

Duncan Robertson stood quietly for a moment, watching the horse saunter off. Then he returned to the spit over the fire, muttering to himself. "Faither should lash him just fer bein' an idiot." As he rotated the meat on the spit, a delicious aroma filled the air.

Abby's stomach growled softly, protesting the lack of food that day. She leaned toward Rory and whispered, "What's that smell, Rory? It's making my mouth water!"

Rory grunted softly in agreement. Keeping his voice low he answered, "It's kinnen. Now I suppose ye want one?"

Abby poked him in the side. "Well...yes, I'm starving. But that's not what we're here to do. If your father's sword is here, where do you think it might be?"

Rory contemplated the question for a moment. "I don't think they'd expect me to come looking for it here, so it may be out in the open." With a quick shrug, he added, "but maybe it's in the house."

Abby eyed the deteriorating building, which seemed ready to fall down at any moment. "Rory, see that hole in the back of the house?" she whispered. "I think I can squeeze through it!"

"What?" With a stern look in his eye, Rory shook his head. "No, it's too dangerous, A-by. Ye should stay hidden in the trees while I search."

Abby stifled a snort. "What do you think I am, Numpty, a helpless, fair maiden? I'll be in and out of that place lickety-split and Duncan Robertson will be none the wiser for it!"

Rory growled under his breath, "Ye'll do no such thing, A-by. That man is dangerous. A distraction is what we need."

Abby shouldered her backpack, and with a stubborn air, turned to face Rory. "A distraction, eh? Well, how about this?!" Abby grabbed Rory's pigtails, pulled herself up onto her tiptoes, and planted a firm kiss on his lips. When she released him, Rory stood motionless, eyes like saucers, dumbfounded. Abby quickly turned and stepped into the shadows before Rory could regain his composure.

10

*A*bby crept silently toward the back of the house, taking great care with each step. Duncan Robertson continued to tend the fire, oblivious to Abby's actions. Having recovered from Abby's sneak attack, Rory stood temporarily helpless as Abby approached the rear of the battered building.

Nearing her destination, Abby stepped onto a pile of pine needles and froze as a sharp crack escaped from beneath her foot. *Drat!* She thought. *There must have been a stick under the needles.* She drew a deep breath, wishing she had been more careful. Looking over her shoulder, she saw Rory standing in a small pool of light. He lifted a finger to his lips and mouthed to her it was okay for the moment; the crackle of the fire had concealed her presence. Releasing her breath slowly, Abby moved forward and began to examine the hole in the back of the house.

Studying the building's construction, Abby ran her fingers over the jagged surface of woven sticks and what looked like dried mud. Excluding the sticks jutting out here and there, she estimated the hole in the back wall to be about two feet high and maybe ten inches wide. It was about three feet off the ground and just big enough for her to squeeze through. Poking her head inside the opening, she was met by a wall of musty stench. She stifled a cough and quickly pulled her head out. *Great, not only do they act like pigs, they smell like them too! And its pitch black in there; I'm definitely going to need some light.*

Abby unzipped her pack and dug for her flashlight, only to stop short with a mental groan. *Fabulous, I must have dropped my flashlight in the cave when Finlay cornered me.* Abby sighed and leaned against the building. *I do have a couple of matches left, but I don't want to use those. And besides, I don't want to risk a fire. Think Abby, think!*

Trying a new approach, Abby stuck her head into the hole again to see if her eyes would adjust to the dark. After a few minutes, when she could still see nothing, she withdrew her head, gasping for fresh air. Then the solution came to her. *Yes!* She triumphantly pulled her smartphone from her bag. *As long as this sucker's charged, that flashlight app should be perfect!*

Powering up the unit, Abby grunted under her breath when only one battery bar flashed on the screen. "I'll have to work fast then," she murmured to herself. Abby scrolled the screen until she located the picture of a light bulb. Being careful not to draw any attention, she stuck the phone into the hole and touched the screen. A dull glow emanated from the device, allowing Abby's first glimpse inside the house. Prepared for the smell this time, Abby stuck her head through the hole and pointed the light directly below. She was relieved to see no obstacles in her immediate path.

Pulling her head from the building and repositioning

her body, Abby carefully stuck her right leg through the hole. Once her foot was planted firmly inside the structure, she bent low and pulled her body through, taking care to avoid the jagged edges of the hole. She reached back to retrieve her bag, shouldered it quietly, and took stock of the room. Shining her light to the opposite wall, Abby saw a solid front door and no windows. *Good,* she thought. *Hopefully that creep won't notice my light!*

She moved slowly inward, directing the light around the one-room house. A simple table and two stools filled the middle of the room. Two wooden bowls, a pot, and chunks of something rotten were scattered across the tabletop. *Eeeww.* She swung the light to her left, feeling it was safe now to begin her search. Various tools hung from the back wall, many of which appeared to be used for fishing. Several woolen blankets were piled on the floor next to a bed of straw. Abby moved around the table with a shiver, keeping her distance from the bed. *I don't even want to know what's living in there!* A large, wooden chest, with a bulging bag sitting on top, was positioned along the side wall to the left of the front door. *Maybe a sack of grain,* Abby thought. *Hmmm...a chest would be a good place to stash a sword.*

Placing her phone on top of the chest, Abby wrapped her arms around the scratchy sack. With effort, she moved the obstacle to the edge of the chest and pushed it off the side. Flinching at the dull thud of the sack hitting the floor, Abby scooped up her light source and began to examine the chest. There was no visible lock, and the lid needed only a little wiggling before giving way.

Abby opened the lid, surprised by what she saw inside. *Well if that's the sword, this was way too easy!* At the bottom lay the lone occupant of the chest. Worn cloth, dyed in several shades of red, was securely wrapped around a long, pointed object. Abby leaned into the chest and wrapped her free hand around what she was confident would be a hilt.

Idiots. That wasn't much of a hiding place. Abby attempted to lift the sword out of the chest with one hand, and was surprised by its weight. Deciding she couldn't pick the sword up one-handed, she moved back to the table, placed her bag on one of the stools, and laid her phone face-up on the table top. Returning to the chest, Abby leaned in and grasped the hilt of the sword with both hands. With a little added muscle, she hoisted the sword in front of her.

Abby doubted either Robertson could use a weapon like this. *It's got to be Rory's father's sword,* she thought. Abby carried the sword to the table, and with her back to the door, held her find over the light to further examine it. She loosened the wrap around the hilt, revealing an ornate handle.

She gasped in shock after closely examining the hilt. A familiar symbol stared back at her. "The Red King," Abby whispered to herself. Millions of thoughts began to scream through her mind. *This makes no sense whatsoever! Why would Rory's father have a sword with the symbol of the Red King on it?*

Movement outside the back of the house snapped Abby from her momentary confusion. "Psst. A-by"

Abby set the sword on the table and pointed her light

toward the hole in the wall, catching a glimpse of Rory's face in the opening. Abby whispered back sternly. "Shhh. Don't make so much noise, Rory."

Rory poked his head through the hole, lowering his voice this time. "A-by, did ye find anythin'?"

Abby replied uncertainly. "Well, yes, I found a sword but I'm not so sure this is the right one."

"Let me see it A-by; put it in the light." Abby lifted the hilt end of the sword off of the table and directed the light down the handle and across the red wrap. Rory bumped his head on the top of the hole in excitement. "It's me faither's sword, A-by! Bring it to me!"

Abby turned the light back to Rory. "Okay, okay, but keep your voice down." Without warning, the phone went black. Abby froze in place. "Great!"

"What happened to the light, A-by?"

"The battery died."

"The ba-ter-e?"

"Never mind, Rory, I'll explain it later. Right now I want to get out of this stink-hole, and fast! I'm surprised Duncan hasn't heard us yet."

"Follow me voice if ye can't see yer way."

"Good idea. Give me just a minute though." Abby laid the sword flat on the table and felt for her backpack in the darkness. Locating the bag, she tucked the phone away and secured the backpack over both shoulders.

Feeling the table again for the hilt of the sword, Abby lifted it upright with both hands, grunting softly from its heft. With the combined weight of the sword and her backpack making her somewhat unsteady, Abby took a step backward to work her way around the table. She immediately realized her mistake when she backed into an unseen object near the front door and began to lose her balance.

Abby screamed silently to herself. *Oh, no! You've got to be kidding!*

Stumbling backwards, she tried to regain her footing, but it was too late. As she toppled over, Abby's backpack hit the front door of the house, flinging it open. She fell through the doorway with a crash, groaning as she landed on her bag.

A sharp pain shot through Abby's back as she froze momentarily, hoping no one would notice her if she held her breath and closed her eyes. Still clutching the sword, which she had managed to protect in the fall, Abby waited for what seemed like an eternity before breathing again. Finally, hearing nothing, she slowly opened her eyes.

As she looked up, the flicker of the campfire revealed she was not alone. Looming over her, stick raised high, was the angry figure of Duncan Robertson.

***

Abby's eyes widened as Duncan's stick cut through the dark night toward her. She instinctively tightened her stomach muscles and rolled away from her attacker, all the while keeping the sword extended in front of her. Drawing a sharp, frightful breath, Abby prepared for the impact, sighing with relief when her backpack took the full brunt of the blow with a loud thwack. Duncan grunted at his miscalculation and raised his stick high again.

Before Abby could react, a fiery streak rounded the

house and tackled Duncan, causing the would-be weapon to fly through the air. Rory and his foe rolled in a tangled mess across the ground, stopping just shy of the campfire. Squirming his way from Rory's grasp, Duncan staggered to his feet, desperately searching the ground for his stick. Pulling his dirk, Rory jumped to a fighting stance and spat with disgust. "Hit a defenseless lass, would ye?"

Abby rose clumsily, fighting the weight of the sword. "Hey! I am not defenseless."

Recovering his stick, Duncan glared at Abby. "A thief is what I see," he sneered, pointing his stick at her.

Rory jumped between Duncan and Abby, dirk held high, ready to lunge. "Ye should no' use such words when ye are exactly what ye speak of! Stand down and we shall leave with what is rightly mine."

Duncan scoffed. "Aye. Ye shall leave, but no' with me treasure."

A growl erupted from deep within Rory's chest. "It's me faither's sword. Ye have no claim to it." Lunging at Duncan with renewed fury, Rory called over his shoulder to Abby. "A-by, go quickly. Take the sword and keep it safe."

Abby refused to budge. "No way, Rory. I'm not leaving you. Besides, that other buffoon still might be out there."

Rory continued to thrust and parry with Duncan, circling the campfire. "Stubborn lass, listen to me for once, please!"

Abby rolled her eyes, grudgingly doing as Rory asked. Lifting the sword in front of her with effort, she rounded the fire opposite the dueling pair and headed away from the camp into dark, new territory. Slowed by the weight of the sword, Abby stumbled into the blackness beyond the fire's glow, fearful of what might lie ahead. Even after her eyes adjusted to the lack of light, all she could see was darkness. Finally, winded from the effort of hefting the sword, Abby stopped to catch her breath at the edge of a small, lone stand of pine trees.

Turning back toward the shack, Abby could see two silhouettes still engaged in combat by the fire. A chilling breeze carried the sounds of grunts and muffled shouts as the men continued to thrust at each other and roll in the dirt. Abby shivered, feeling uncertain. *Should I go back, despite what Rory said? I could hide the sword here. But how could I help, anyway, without a weapon?*

Abby heard branches rustle behind her. Heart pounding, she jumped and clamped a hand over her mouth, muffling a small squeak. *Well this is ridiculous! No telling who else might be out here in the woods. With my luck, Banner Robertson has fallen drunk from his horse and will awake at any moment. He could squish me to death if I didn't see him coming!*

Deciding that returning to Rory would be better than standing alone in the dark, Abby laid the sword on the ground next to the base of a tree and concealed it with pine needles. *Sorry Rory, you're just going to have to be mad at me!* She slipped an arm from her backpack and swung it to the ground, resting the bag on top of the sword as a marker. *That will have to do.*

Abby quickly retraced her steps to the edge of the Robertson's camp and hid in the shadows. Rory and his adversary remained in a heated skirmish around the fire. Rory jumped from the reach of Duncan's stick. "Why did ye destroy me hame?"

Duncan cackled, "It was no' me plan." He jabbed his stick at Rory, again narrowly missing. "But when me clumsy oaf of a brother dropped his lantern, seemed the perfect way to rid our lands of MacKay filth once and fer all."

"Me family is no' filth!" Rage burned through Rory's eyes as he feverishly lunged at Duncan, this time miscalculating the swing of his challenger's stick. The weapon connected with Rory's ribs with a loud crack. "Oof." Rory dropped to the ground, grabbing his midsection. Duncan continued with force, delivering a second blow to Rory's back.

Crouched at the edge of camp, Abby gasped, frantically thinking of a way to help Rory. Then it came to her.

Staying in the shadows, Abby circled the perimeter to the back of the hut and quickly slipped through the hole in the wall. The front door stood open, letting in just enough light from the fire to guide her way. Abby could see Duncan lifting his stick for what looked like a blow to Rory's head.

Without hesitating, Abby grabbed the pot from the table, jumped over the sack of grain, and dashed through the door. She approached Duncan from behind, calling out, "Hey! Meatball!"

Startled, Duncan stopped mid swing, then turned to see where the voice came from. He stood immobile for a moment, just long enough for Abby to close the distance between them and crack him over the head with the pot. He instantly crumpled to the ground.

Abby looked down at the groaning man and grinned. *So there. Serves you right!*

Rushing to Rory's side, Abby discarded the pot and knelt to inspect his wounds. "Are you okay, Rory?" Rory stared in disbelief at his companion. Abby shrugged. "What? It worked for your mom!"

Rory snorted in satisfaction but then grimaced and grabbed his ribs. Abby frowned. "Anything broken?"

"No, but will need time to heal."

Hearing Duncan moan again, Abby extended her hand to Rory. "Come on. We better get out of here before he comes to."

"Aye." Rory nodded, slowly getting to his feet. With a concerned look in his eye, Rory paused. "Is me faither's sword safe, A-by?"

Abby motioned for Rory to hurry up. "Don't worry. I hid it at the edge of camp."

Rory gathered his composure and tucked his dirk in its sheath. "Thanks for coming back, A-by."

Abby smirked. "No problem, Numpty. We really need to get going though." This time, Abby took Rory by the arm and guided him in the right direction.

Rory hesitated. "Wait, A-by."

"Are you crazy? We need to leave...now!"

Rory slipped from Abby's arm and hurried to the fire. He grabbed the spit with the kinnen and returned to her side, grinning from ear to ear.

"What? We need to eat."

11

"*R*ory, are you sure that leather strap will hold the sword on your back? Looks a bit flimsy to me."

Rory grunted, handing Abby another chunk of kinnen as they followed the tree line away from the Robertson camp. Despite his injuries and the weight of the sword, Rory navigated the terrain quickly, challenging Abby to keep up.

Chewing while she walked, Abby savored the spit-roasted rabbit. "I never thought I'd say this, Rory, but kinnen is delicious." She wiped her fingers on her backpack and took a swig from her water bottle. "Thanks for catching one for us!"

Rory turned and smiled. "Aye, and I caught him already cooked."

Shaking the water bottle, Abby held it up to the moonlight to check the contents. "Well, now we're almost out of water."

"Don't worry, A-by. I know where to get some."

Abby frowned skeptically. "Great, as long as it isn't like the last water you found for us, lead the way."

Rory headed away from the tree line and onto the open mountain side, leading Abby higher and higher up the steep incline. After an hour or so, she guessed they must be far enough from the Robertson camp to stop looking over her shoulder. Ignoring signs of thirst and exhaustion, she forged ahead, determined to keep pace with Rory.

Finally, Rory stopped and pointed off in the distance. "Beyond that hill is a spring of fresh water. We can rest there. Can ye keep goin' a bit further, A-by?"

"For fresh water? Most definitely!" With a renewed surge of energy, Abby charged ahead of Rory to the top of the hill. Her hair danced in the cool breeze that greeted her as she crested the lower portion of the mountainside. In the distance, she could just make out hints of what looked like a well. Moonlight outlined smooth stones in a circular pattern standing about two feet high.

Rory caught up to Abby at the top of the rise. "So, I see yer not so tired after all, A-by." He cocked his head and grinned. "But can ye keep up with me?"

Rory sprinted down the hill and off toward the well, arriving far ahead of Abby. Hurriedly removing the sword from his back, he sat on the stone wall and leaned over the side to drink. Chills ran down Abby's spine. "Rory! Stop!" she screamed abruptly. "Are you sure that's safe?"

Rory cupped his hands and brought the liquid to his mouth, drinking deeply. "Aye. Ye see, A-by? Good, clear water." Rory smiled, then suddenly leaped up and began staggering about, clasping both hands to his throat. Horrific gargling sounds emitted from deep within Rory's chest as he twisted in mid-air, paused for a moment, and collapsed to the ground.

"Rory!" Abby shrieked and rushed to Rory's side, finding him still as could be, staring off into the dark night. She rolled Rory onto his back and shook his shoulders with force. "Rory, can you hear me?" When she received no response, Abby placed her ear over his mouth and nose. *Oh no! I don't think he's breathing! Okay. Stay calm...give him some air.*

Abby tipped Rory's head back and opened his airway, wishing she had done more than just look at pamphlets about CPR. Closing Rory's nose, Abby blew two deep breaths into his mouth. She drew back and examined him. With no apparent change, she pinched Rory's nose again and began to deliver another deep breath. This time Abby received a reaction, but not the one she was expecting. As she began to pull away, Rory simultaneously slipped a hand behind her neck and kissed her, then erupted in to a fit of laughter.

Abby pulled away from Rory and jumped to her feet, delivering a swift kick to his shin. "That wasn't funny, Numpty!"

Rubbing his assaulted leg and grasping his injured ribs, Rory caught his breath, pulled himself from the ground, and reached for Abby's hand. "I didn't mean to scare ye, A-by."

Abby brushed Rory's hand away and sat on the edge of the well, turning her back to him. "I wasn't scared. Just... just don't do that again! Got it?"

Rory sat beside Abby and placed a gentle hand on her shoulder. "A-by, I'm sorry."

After a silent moment, Abby shrugged and turned to face Rory. "I wasn't afraid the water was poisoned, or anything." She paused, then continued quietly. "You see, my mom died by falling into a well. So, that just freaked me out a little, you know?"

Rory groaned. "Oh, A-by, please forgive me. I am a stupit lad sometimes."

Abby smiled. "It's okay." She pulled the empty water bottle from her bag. "Look, let's fill up and find somewhere a little safer to rest."

Rory hopped atop the well wall and began walking its perimeter, demonstrating its safety. "Don't worry A-by. Nothin' bad can happen here, if ye believe the stories."

Abby raised a curious eyebrow as she filled her water bottle. "What stories?"

Rory jumped down and gestured to the well. "It's said this well is enchanted," he whispered mysteriously. "Every year, 'bout this time, plain young girls come to sing and dance around the well 'til they fall fast asleep from exhaustion." Rory laid against the well and pretended to snore. After a few seconds, he opened his eyes and stretched his arms, batting his eyelashes. "Then when they awake the next morn' . . ." Rory leaped to his feet and smiled, posing with hands on hips. "They are transformed into beautiful maidens!" Rory held the pose and peaked at Abby to see if she was smiling.

Abby snickered. "Sounds a bit unbelievable, if you ask me."

"As unbelievable as a talking dog?" He picked up the sword and slung it across his back again.

Abby groaned. "Point taken. Still, sounds like a fairytale. So, I suppose the well has some kind of magical name then, huh?"

Rory scratched his head for a moment. "Aye. It's called the Well of Fare Maidens."

Grabbing Abby by the hand, Rory set off with purpose. "Come, A-by. There's a cave nearby. We can light a fire; ye will feel safer there."

Abby reluctantly followed, a stray thought bouncing in the back of her mind as they continued climbing the mountainside. *Why do I feel like I've heard that name before?*

As Rory led her to the mouth of the cave, Abby gasped, recalling her conversation with Mrs. MacTavish. *That's where my mom died!*

***

Abby slumped against the mouth of the cave, gazing out into the moonlight at the mysterious well. *Could that really be where my mom died? This just doesn't make sense. I need to investigate that well, but Rory will probably throw a fit if I tell him why.*

Rory worked diligently behind Abby to build a fire with pieces of a gnarled, dead tree from just outside the cave entrance. Taking note of his struggle to ignite the pile of wood, Abby produced her box of matches. "Here Rory, let me help."

Rory sheepishly allowed Abby to start the fire. "Thanks, A-by."

Rory leaned over the small fire. Placing his father's sword in his lap, he began tracing the symbols along the blade with his finger. Abby plopped to the ground and watched him in silence, wrestling with a nagging thought.

"Rory?"

Rory stopped and met Abby's eyes. "Aye, A-by?"

"Don't you find it odd Finlay brought me here to find the Red King and you're sitting with a sword in your lap that bears his symbols?"

Rory snorted. "These are the symbols of me faither's family, no' the Red King!"

Abby shook her head. "Rory, I've seen that symbol in several places. In a book in my father's library, carved on a stone near the base of this mountain, and..." Abby gasped, remembering the scroll.

Abby snatched up her backpack and rummaged through a deep, zippered pouch until she wrapped her hands around the soft leather. She pulled the scroll out with care. "And in here!"

With a skeptical look on his face, Rory scooted around the fire to get a closer look. "Where did ye get that, A-by?"

"I found it in a hidden hole, deep in the back of a cave around the other side of the mountain, except, in my time. In fact, right before Finlay dropped me on top of you."

Abby gingerly unrolled the leather and pulled it taut, tilting it just right so the flickers of the flames illuminated the strange writing. "See, at the top of the scroll. That's the symbol of the Red King, the same symbol I keep seeing. Now look at your sword."

Rory held the sword flat on the top of his palms and examined the symbols. With a loud grunt, he nodded slowly. "Aye, A-by. The markings are the same."

The pair sat quiet for several minutes, contemplating the meaning of their discovery. Recognizing Rory's internal struggle, Abby redirected his focus. "Rory, can you read this writing?"

Rory slowly pulled his eyes away from the fire and

took the scroll from Abby. After a brief moment, Rory responded with a touch of disbelief. "Aye, A-by. I can't believe it, but this is the song me mither sang to me as a child. She had the writing of it in Gaelic, passed down from me faither's faither."

"Well," piped Abby eagerly, "what does it say? In English? Can you translate it for me?"

Rory cleared his throat and began to sing in hushed tones the same, haunting melody he had hummed when his home was destroyed. He began tentatively, translating a word at a time, building tempo as the lyrics returned to him, then tapered off as if overwhelmed by sadness.

> Green tendrils reign
> Engulf the land
> A rightful warrior
> Will come again.
> Heart and hand
> Head of fire
> A just, true soul
> Regains the power.
> A golden drop
> The third of three
> Bears the power
> To set them free.
> Fools beware
> Rethink your hate
> 'Ere fire binds gold
> To seal your fate.

The last word rolled from Rory's mouth in but a whisper. Abby sat mesmerized by the song. "It is the same," Rory acknowledged softly. "Word for word."

Coming to her senses, Abby dug into her bag and produced a small notepad and pen. "Rory, will you say the words again, slowly? I want to write them down so I can study them."

Rory nodded and spoke the puzzling words. When he finished, he looked to Abby. "What do ye think it means, A-by?"

Abby sat thoughtfully for a moment, then stretched out on her stomach and tapped a boot on the cave floor. "Well..." Abby stared at her English version. "Sounds like a prophecy to me. It was probably set to music sometime after it was written, to help people remember it. How about we break it down, section by section?"

Rory nodded as he joined Abby, stretching his slender yet muscular frame in front of the fire.

> Green tendrils reign
> Engulf the land
> A rightful warrior
> Will come again.

Abby continued to thump the toe of her boot. "I'm not sure what this business about green tendrils is, but the part about the warrior is straight forward enough. Someone with the right to some type of power, maybe, will come to free the land."

> Heart and hand
> Head of fire
> A just, true soul
> Regains the power.

"Hmmm. The first two lines are a bit tricky, but the rightful warrior must have a true, or pure soul...be a good person, to regain whatever the power is."

Abby watched Rory out of the corner of her eye as he once again traced the symbols on the sword. His hair mirrored the fiery red of the deepest, flickering flames. *Head of fire...I wonder.*

A golden drop
The third of three
Bears the power
To set them free.

"This part is pretty confusing. A golden drop? Of what? Does it mean actual gold? Or something the color of gold? And is it the third of three golden drops, or does it maybe mean the third of some object, person, or action?" Abby groaned. "Well whatever it is, it can set someone free."

Fools beware
Rethink your hate
'Ere fire binds gold
To seal your fate.

"Sounds like this means some hateful fools better watch their step. I wonder what their fate would be though. Pretty vague, if you ask me." Abby stared into the fire and yawned.

Rory cleared his throat and stared at the cave floor, momentarily lost in memory. "Me mither told me a story bout' the Red King when I was just a lad."

Surprised, Abby shifted to face Rory and interrupted speculatively, "But you didn't believe it, right, because you think it's all 'rubbish?'"

Rory shrugged with a new uncertainty. "The Red King was said to be in love with a beautiful maiden named Enya, the daughter of a powerful magician. Enya's faither forged a sword unlike any other sword and entrusted it to the Red King. This sword could counter the strongest of faerie magic, but the magician still feared for the safety of his beloved daughter and the child she was due to bare. On his death bed, Enya's faither bestowed a powerful magic to her, one as powerful and brilliant as the sun above. He told her to remember 'with light comes freedom' and 'a grand unjust' would be righted. Those were the last words to escape his mouth."

Abby traced the symbols on the sword with her eyes, stopping when she came to a curious inset at the bottom of the hilt she had not yet noticed. The shape seemed oddly familiar to her, but she could not place it. Abby whispered the phrase to herself, "with light comes freedom." With a furrowed brow, she looked to Rory. "What do you think he meant by that?"

"Time to rest, A-by...we shall worry 'bout the meaning later." Rory yawned and scooted closer to the fire. "Besides, we need our strength to find the Red King," he added, cradling the sword close to his chest. "Ye helped me get me faither's sword, now I shall keep me word."

Abby placed the scroll and notepad back in her bag and curled up on the other side of the fire on the hard cave floor. *Sure Rory, we need our strength to find the Red King. But I don't think we will have to look much further. I think I may have already found him!*

12

*A*bby awoke several hours later to the soft sounds of Rory snoring. His arm was draped over the mysterious sword, which seemed to reflect the colors of the fire with great intensity. Finding it odd the fire still burned bright, Abby outstretched her hands to welcome its warmth. After soaking in the heat for several minutes, Abby stood and gathered her bag in silence. *Rory is sleeping soundly, perfect time to go check out that well without him badgering me. A quick walk-around for any clues and I'll be back before he wakes.*

Abby tip-toed to the mouth of the cave and looked over her shoulder one last time to assure herself Rory did not stir. She held her breath and slipped out of the cave and down the mountain side. The morning sun eased its way above the dark tree line in the distance, giving Abby the light she needed to quickly find her way to the well.

The well looked different to Abby with the warm glow of sunshine creeping up its base. Bright green moss covered the face of the stones. Abby placed her backpack on the ground and sat on the edge of the well, running her hand over the fuzzy moss. Thumbing her mother's amulet, Abby thought of the night Sage had given it to her – a night that now seemed like so many months ago. She also thought about Mrs. McTavish's story of the Well of Fair Maidens. Could this really be where her mother died? Abby stared at her reflection in the water. The dark liquid glistened as the sun's rays stretched out to touch its surface. Cupping her hands, Abby brought the cool, crisp water to her mouth and drank deeply. "I wish you were still here, Mom." Abby took a second helping of water. "I wish I had been able to know you...to have had you kiss me goodnight and read me stories. You don't have to worry though; Sage has been a great big-sister."

After several quiet minutes, Abby sighed, stood, and circled the well, examining every stone for anything unusual. Finding nothing out of sorts, she turned her back to the structure and surveyed the surrounding landscape. Wildflowers spotted the hillside, with an occasional bush or tree breaking the smooth line of the horizon.

Frustrated she wasn't finding any clues, Abby turned back to the well and placed her hands on top of the stones as she leaned over to stare deep into the water's depths. "I could sure use a sign here, Mom. This whole thing is crazy. A talking dog takes me through a time warp, tells me I have to find the Red King, and drops me on top of a Scotsman who clearly doesn't realize his family history." Abby added with a whisper, "And I have no idea how and if I will ever get back home."

Squeezing her eyes tight, Abby took in a deep breath. Upon doing so, a hint of filth and grime worked its way into her nostrils. Abby crinkled her nose in disgust and opened her eyes. Her reflection was no longer the only one looking back at her from the water's surface.

Abby gasped as she recognized the smelly thief from the forest, the one she had blasted with pepper spray. Before she could turn around, the thief shoved a dirty cloth gag into her mouth and wrapped his greasy arms around her waist. She attempted to scream but was countered by a second person pulling a wool sack over her head. "Oh great!" she tried to exclaim through the gag, without success. *That must be the thief that fought with Rory!*

Abby kicked and wriggled with all her might. She tried to scream, but her protests were muffled by the gag and the sack. She felt her arms and legs being bound with thick, rough rope, and then heard a familiar, raspy voice buzzing in her ear. "Ye may scream all ye want, Witch. Will do no good. We 'ave ye now." Abby felt the second set of hands hoist her aloft and fling her over a huge, beefy shoulder.

Contorting her body like a caterpillar, Abby kicked aimlessly into the air. She tried helplessly to call out to Rory but knew her efforts were useless. *This is not good! I've got a bad, bad feeling. No telling where these pigs are taking me or what they have planned. How is Rory going to find me? Or will he even try?*

"Don't forget the Witch's bag," said the man who was carrying her.

"Aye," replied the stinky man. "No tellin' what the feisty lass may 'ave in it."

Abby squirmed and kicked in a final protest as she felt the motion of long strides. Stinky – as she chose to think of him - poked at her back. "Ye best behave an' try no tricks, Witch. Ar' Masters will 'ave none of that and ye don't want to make them mad."

Masters? Oh no, that must mean they are taking me to Mavis and Tavis!

***

Abby thought the queasy motion induced by the beefy man's lumbering steps would never end. To her relief, she finally felt herself being lowered to the ground. Her captor dropped her the last few inches, as if to let her know who was in charge, and her back smacked against a cold, hard wall. The two thieves traded jumbled whispers before suddenly ripping the woolen sack from Abby's head. Abby let out a muffled shriek as the rough fibers burned into her face. As her eyes adjusted to the dim surroundings, she wondered what the thieves were arguing about.

A heavy, damp darkness seemed to permeate the place, and Abby hoped she wouldn't be abandoned there alone. From somewhere in the distance, a pulsing, green glow faintly emanated, giving Abby a false moment of hope that Finlay was coming to help her. *I must be in a cave again,* she thought. *But I can't believe how dark it is! And if that glow isn't from Finlay, I don't think I want to know where it's coming from!*

A brilliant burst of flames erupted near Abby's face. Blinded for many moments by the makeshift torch in front of her, Abby felt the rotten rag being loosened and pulled from her mouth. Between the smell of the sack and the taste of the rag, it was all Abby could do not to vomit. She cleared her throat and spat what fibrous remnants she could toward the flames. "I need a drink of water," she said, her voice cracking.

A growl came from behind the flames. "No, Witch. All ye need is to do as yer told. Ar' Masters will come for ye soon."

Abby scowled and imagined the pompous thieves' heads inflated like balloons begging to burst. What she would give for a pin to pop them. She sighed and leaned against the cave wall. "Will you at least untie me? The ropes are hurting me."

The men turned away and traded argumentative whispers again for several minutes. Abby thought she could pick out the words 'reward', 'skewer her', and 'punishment'. Returning to Abby, the stinky man drew a dirk from his ragged belt. Abby gasped and scooted away, unsure of his intentions.

The beefy man jabbed the torch toward Abby's side. "Hold still, Witch. Ye wan' yer legs free or no'?" Abby flinched and recoiled from the sudden heat. She held her breath while the man holding the knife leaned over and severed the rope around her ankles. As her bindings fell to the floor, Abby breathed a sigh of relief, holding back both her fear and anger. "Thanks, Stinky" she muttered under her breath.

"What's that?" The man eyed her suspiciously, still pointing the knife in her direction.

"Nothing." Abby pursed her lips. "Nothing at all."

"Yer darn right, yer nothing at all, Witch." The beefy man glared threateningly at her. "No wild ideas, either. Ye run, ye won't get far."

Abby stretched her legs and rotated her ankles in hopes of working out the stiffness, just in case she had the chance to run. But her entire body ached and she was sure she wouldn't be able to move fast enough to escape even if she saw an opportunity. The gravity of the situation began to weigh upon her and she began to fear for the worst.

After a few more minutes of continued argument between the two thieves, noises came from deep inside the cave. Abby looked toward the faint, green glow and then to her captors. The men immediately fell silent as they retreated to the other side of the chamber, holding the torch behind their backs.

Abby called out to the men. "Hey! Where are you going? What's happening?" When she didn't receive a reply from the thieves, Abby struggled to her feet. A cold chill ran up her spine when the noises turned into voices. Abby gulped as two figures materialized in a brilliant, green glow. *Mavis and Tavis.*

***

A throbbing, green orb flew through the chamber toward the thieves and smashed against the wall. Green sparks showered down upon the men, sizzling as they touched their flesh. "Fools!" A green-skinned figure prepared to lob another orb toward the men.

The beefy man shrieked in horror and dropped his torch on the ground. Stinky danced on top of it to extinguish the flames as his partner professed many urgent apologies, muttering, "We had to be able to keep an eye on 'er!" Gesturing toward Abby, Stinky whined, "It was dark!"

The second green-skinned figure moved ominously toward the men. "Don't make us remind you again. No fire! Next time..." The mysterious figure caught a glimpse of Abby from the corner of his eye and immediately turned to face her. A ball of green energy formed in his hand and he daintily flicked it to the ceiling. Green tendrils emerged from the ball and rapidly engulfed the entire room, creating an electric glow in the chamber. "Mavis," said the second figure with a smile, "come here, Brother."

The first figure wafted to his brother's side. "Well, well, Tavis, what treasure did you find us?"

Mavis and Tavis closed the space between themselves and Abby with freakish speed. The tall, lean figures appeared to glide across the floor. Abby pressed against the cave wall and grimaced, wishing her hands were free as she mashed them between her back and the rough cave wall.

The surreal forms stood to either side of Abby and examined her carefully. Abby examined them back, noting the two figures looked almost identical except for their eye and hair color. The figure identified as Mavis – who had thrown the glowing electric orb at the thieves – had the spookiest eyes she had ever seen. His black pupils were surrounded by an even blacker, thick iris, creating the impression of two deep, dark, evil pits in his face. His short, blond hair stood haphazardly on end, reaching in every direction for the ceiling. In contrast, the figure called Tavis had black, slicked-back hair and sparkling green eyes that matched his skin, adding to the elegance of his carriage.

A knot formed in Abby's stomach as Mavis stroked the

blond curl that dangled on her forehead. "Hmmm," he grinned, revealing pointed teeth that made Abby's knees knock. "I think we'll keep this one, Brother." With Mavis nearly drooling on her, Abby wondered if she was going to be the main course for dinner. Taking a deep breath, she gathered the bravest voice she could. "Um, Sirs? Would you mind terribly freeing my hands? These ropes are hurting me."

Faster than Abby's eyes could follow, Mavis withdrew his hand and lobbed a green orb at the thieves. It stopped abruptly a foot in front of them and hovered in the air, twitching back and forth, eager to find its targets. Tavis cocked his head at the miscreants, "How dare you treat our guest with such disregard."

"We had to bind 'er," cried Stinky. "A witch she is!"

Tavis glared at the men and nodded to Mavis to release the orb, which fell harmlessly to the floor of the cave. Turning his attention back to Abby, Tavis lifted a long, crooked finger and with the slightest flick, lobbed a tiny green ball behind Abby's back, severing the ropes that bound her. Abby brought her arms forward and flinched as she rubbed her wrists. "Th-thanks," she whispered.

"There, there," said Tavis with a charming smile that revealed perfect, glistening teeth. Reaching down gallantly, he drew Abby's hand to his lips and planted a soft kiss on top. "Please accept our most humble apologies, my dear. These fools will inconvenience you no more."

Tavis released Abby's hand and stood to his full height, which Abby estimated to be a little more than six feet. He looked to Mavis and motioned with a flick of the head over his shoulder toward the thieves. Mavis grinned and wrung his hands together as he glided within inches of the cowering men. Stinky tried to hide behind Beefy as an orb formed in each of Mavis's palms. "M-master," cried Stinky from behind his grimy counterpart, "may we 'ave our reward?"

Mavis cackled and flicked both orbs above the thieves, causing them to cower further and cover their heads. The orbs collided and showered the men in green sparks. Stinky and Beefy began to scream but stopped short when they realized the sparks were turning to coins. The men, giddy with relief, began scooping up the coins and dumping them into the sack that had served as Abby's blindfold. Mavis sneered at the men and began forming another, flickering orb. "Be gone," he commanded as he raised the ball of sparks to eye level.

Stinky and Beefy stopped in their tracks and raised their heads to meet the orb. "Aye, Master," groveled Stinky as he scooped up one last handful of coins. Beefy slung the bag over his shoulder and pushed his way past his partner, desperate to get out of the cave. Stinky tossed Abby's backpack toward the figures, muttering, "Here are the witch's charms," before slinking away.

As the thieves fled the chamber, Mavis turned his attention back to Abby, closing the space between them faster than she cared for. "What say you, Brother? She bears the mark."

Tavis considered his brother's words and put an arm around Abby's back as Mavis picked up Abby's backpack and stepped to her other side. "Dear maiden, we do apologize for the hasty and cruel manner that has brought you to our abode." Tavis exchanged a knowing glance with

Mavis as he continued speaking. "Would you be so kind as to accompany us to our special chamber? We have a job for you of the utmost importance."

Before Abby could respond, the brothers whisked her into the tunnel at an alarming rate. The temperature dropped precipitously, giving Abby goose bumps. As they flew deeper and deeper inside, Abby began to feel the tunnel closing in around her. The only thing she could manage to do was call out in her mind, *Finlay!*

13

*T*he tunnel seemed endless to Abby. A faint, green glow covered all surfaces, allowing her enough light to examine her captors more closely. Both figures wore jet-black tunics and tight, green leggings, the hue a shade darker than their glistening skin. Mavis was the same height as Tavis, dwarfing Abby's petite frame. Except for the color of their skin, their ability to float about flinging green balls of energy, and Mavis's alarming eyes, they appeared 'human-like' to her. Yet, they certainly weren't human.

Hmm. Abby forgot her fear for a moment as she puzzled out the nature of the creatures. She thought of her mother's hidden book, telling of faeries with green skin that captured humans in Caledonia, never to be seen again. *But aren't faeries small and cute, with lacy wings and pointy ears?* Abby wondered. She glanced up again at the figures whisking her through the tunnel. *No pointy ears.* They bore no resemblance to any faerie Abby had ever imagined. But they did look like the strange green beings dancing on the cover of her mother's book.

Wow. Abby gasped audibly. *These guys must be the twin faerie brothers whose existence Rory insisted was "rubbish." These are the guys from the book! The ones that use a magical dog to kidnap young girls.* Abby felt sick thinking Finlay was her kidnapper. It made sense though; his fur was the same green as the faeries' skin. *Hasn't Finlay been trying to help me though? Or has he just been trying to help himself to be set free?* She wondered for a minute if Finlay had tricked her into this dangerous situation. And where was Rory when she needed him? Maybe he would never find her in the depths of this dank fortress. Abby swallowed hard, hoping she was not about to disappear forever.

Clearing her mind, Abby saw the tunnel was beginning to glow brighter and brighter, so much so she nearly had to shut her eyes. She could see an opening up ahead, from which a blinding golden light overpowered the green of the tunnel. The faeries brought Abby to an abrupt halt when they reached the source of the pulsating glow, hesitating to step into the space beyond.

Cringing momentarily, Mavis and Tavis crossed the threshold into an enormous chamber that seemed almost alive with its intense incandescence. A steep, twisting trail led some seventy yards to a pair of what Abby thought must be stone chairs in the middle of the cavern floor below. Looking around, it dawned on her something wasn't quite right with the walls and ceiling of the chamber. *What in the world*, she thought, squinting into the bright, golden hue. She wasn't certain, but there appeared to be sets of green eyes spattered everywhere, all staring back at her. No matter where Abby looked, she saw the same 'eyes' peering back. Abby focused in on one spot and gasped, blurting out, "Are those faeries trapped in the walls?"

"Yes, yes, my dear," replied Tavis, motioning as if to wipe a tear from his eye. "They are our brethren."

"An appalling sight," spat Mavis with a look of disgust.

Abby stood silent, her mouth agape as she scanned the cavern. Hundreds upon hundreds of faeries appeared frozen in place just inside the surface of the walls and ceiling, like prehistoric insects frozen in time inside a huge chunk of amber. The brothers allowed Abby to take in the surroundings for only a moment. They abruptly scooped her up, each hoisting an arm, and whisked her down the trail, stopping in front of the stone chairs.

Mavis placed Abby's backpack on the ground and motioned for Tavis to take one of the seats. "Brother..."

Tavis shook his head and with an exaggerated swoop of his arm, indicated that Mavis should sit. "No, no, dear brother, after you. I do insist."

Mavis bowed to Tavis and took his seat. As he placed his hands on the arms of the chair, green tendrils began to encapsulate the throne, casting an electric, green glow that outshone even the golden hue from above. Tavis smiled in approval and sat in the adjacent chair, majestically sparking it to life as well. Many silent moments passed as the faeries eyed Abby, Mavis wringing his hands and Tavis stroking his chin.

The silence was killing Abby, not to mention the indescribable look on Mavis's face. She cleared her throat and asked politely. "Sirs? May I ask why there are faeries stuck in the walls?"

The brothers looked at each other, surprised by Abby's controlled demeanor. Mavis motioned with his hand for Tavis to answer.

Tavis stroked his chin once more for good measure and leaned forward in his throne, locking eyes with Abby. "Interesting you should ask, my dear." Tavis flicked a green ball from hand to hand. "The answer to your question is in fact the very reason you are here. We require your assistance with this most unfortunate situation."

***

Abby gulped and considered what the strange creature had just said to her. Thinking it best to continue being polite, Abby took a deep breath and replied. "Exactly how do you expect me to assist you with this 'unfortunate situation'? I'm uncertain of what I could possibly do to help you?"

Mavis sneered and flicked an orb the size of a marble toward Abby's head. Abby gasped and flinched backward as the ball stopped abruptly level with her forehead. Energy crackled around Abby's head and she feared her hair might start on fire if the orb came any closer.

"Do not play ignorant with us," cackled Mavis. "You bear the mark; you must be the gifted one."

Abby stuttered with confusion, "What mark...what do you mean 'the gifted one'?"

Tavis motioned to his brother and the green orb fell to the ground, bursting into little green sparks as it collided with the cavern floor. Tavis then stood and floated to stop in front of Abby. He raised a hand to briefly stroke her chin. The unexpected chill from his fingers caused Abby to clench her teeth. "There, there. Don't be frightened, my dear." Tavis lifted Abby's chin until her eyes met his. He then brushed his hand slowly up her cheek to the sole blond ringlet in her chestnut hair. He seemed to nearly fall into a trance as he swirled the curl around a slender finger.

Tavis began to speak in a different language. The foreign words rolled elegantly from his tongue. Somehow though, they seemed familiar to Abby. Tavis continued to wrap her golden lock around his finger and spoke the words again, this time in English. "A golden drop, the third of three, bears the power to set them free." Abby gasped. *That's part of the prophecy from the scroll I found! How do the faeries know about it? Are they the ones who wrote it? They must think the 'golden drop' is my golden curl. But what could possibly have given them that idea? That doesn't make any sense.*

"Tavis, Sir," Abby said, clearing her throat. "I don't understand. Is that supposed to be some kind of prophecy? What's the golden drop and what does it have to do with me?"

Tavis continued to twirl Abby's hair around his finger. "You need not worry yourself with the particulars, my dear. Can you not feel the power flowing through your veins? Even our bumbling thieves recognized what you possess."

Abby took a deep, brave breath and tilted her head away from Tavis's hand, stepping backward simultaneously. "All due respect, Sir, but I prefer to worry myself with the particulars. Your two knuckleheads brought me here against my will, and they weren't very nice about it. I think I deserve to know what's going on!"

Mavis hissed in the background as Tavis chuckled eerily. "There, there, Dear. I will favor you with a few answers, but then you will do as you're told." Tavis leaned in toward Abby and stared deep into her eyes. "Agreed?"

Abby gulped, realizing the seriousness of the situation. "Yes, Sir."

Satisfied, Tavis broke eye contact with Abby and floated back to his throne. "So tell me, my dear, what would you like to know?"

Abby thought carefully about what questions she wanted answers to. *I probably shouldn't mention anything about Finlay to them. It's better if they don't know I have any kind of connection with him. But, on the other hand, I still don't know the real reason of why Finlay brought me here...maybe I could get some information out of these creeps. Hmm. Finlay told me his version of what happened to the faeries, maybe hearing what they have to say about it would give me some more clues. But then there's this whole prophecy thing. I really need to figure out what this 'golden drop, third of three' thing means!* Abby breathed deep once again. "I would like to know why your faerie friends are stuck in the walls, please."

Mavis sneered, showing a glimpse of his pointy teeth, as Tavis leaned forward and began to rub his chin again. "Very well," answered Tavis after several silent moments. "Years ago a dreadful wizard..." Tavis trailed off, motioning to Mavis, "What was his name again, dear brother, Fog something?"

Mavis cackled as he wrung his hands, "Myst!"

Tavis shook his head theatrically, "Yes, yes, Brother, that's correct, Sylvan Myst." Tavis turned his attention back to Abby. "You see, a despicable man named Sylvan Myst made it his goal to punish all of our kind." Tavis rose from his throne and glided to the wall of eyes. A green crackle of energy spread from his hand to the wall, masking the golden hue where he stood. Stroking his hand gently over an embedded faerie, he continued. "The good faerie folk of Caledonia lived peacefully, side-by-side, with humans for many centuries. We shared our music and dance, and sometimes magic. The humans, one in particular, loved us dearly... an exquisite beauty like no other." Tavis removed his hand from the wall and in a flash stood before Abby.

Abby recoiled in surprise. "An exquisite beauty, eh?"

Tavis stretched a single finger toward Abby's golden curl. "Why yes, my dear, her beauty was matched by no other. However, I do say you possess a small likeness to her." Tavis stopped short of wrapping the curl around his finger. Restraint was visible in his shaking hand.

Abby chuckled nervously, "A small likeness to her, huh? Who was she?"

Tavis lowered his hand. "Enya, Sylvan Myst's daughter."

Abby raised a mental eyebrow. "I bet he didn't like that much."

Tavis floated back to his throne. "Myst craved power. He was jealous of our remarkable abilities and forbade his daughter any connection with us."

Mavis wrung his hands and spat on the chamber floor. "He hated us so." Abby flinched when Mavis bared his pointy teeth. "A red filth he summoned to the land to destroy us. Myst called him the Red King." A tiny ball of energy formed in Mavis's hand. He flicked the ball into the air where it hung seemingly in suspension some twenty feet off the ground. Abby eyed the ping-pong sized bug zapper nervously as Mavis continued to speak, his voice filled with hatred. "Myst underestimated the power of our numbers though, didn't he brother?"

Tavis nodded. "He certainly did, brother."

Abby swore a glob of drool dripped from Mavis's mouth. "Upon a great rock we slew Myst's red terror."

Tavis smiled eerily at the memory. "The decrepit wizard vowed to rid the countryside of us when learning of our grand victory. Upon his death bed, he cast a hideous spell. My esteemed brother and I escaped only because we were disposing of the remnants of this so-called King."

Mavis leaned forward in his throne, waving his arms in the air. Abby swore it looked like his head was going to explode from anger. "And here you see the results. Putrid. Deceitful. Myst!"

Unexpectedly to Abby, the buzzing ball exploded above them. Thousands of sparkling green bits rained down upon the chamber floor. Abby crouched low and pulled her hood over her head for protection. When the last of the bits sizzled into nothing, Abby warily stood and pulled her hood back. "Well, I...I guess I can see why you both are so angry."

Tavis stroked his chin. "Indeed, my dear."

Abby asked cautiously, "so what did you do with the Red King after you killed him?"

Mavis growled and threw a wave of green energy against the cavern floor. "Enough questions!"

Tavis placed a hand on Mavis's shoulder. "There,

there, Brother...in due time." Tavis focused on Abby. "Please excuse the excitement, my dear, patience has been lacking of late. To answer your question, we burned his body and buried the sword he carried where it will never be found." Tavis then stood and glided to Abby's side. "Now, it is time for you to do what you were brought here to do."

A trickle of sweat worked its way down Abby's spine. *This is most definitely not good. How the heck am I going to get out of here? I have no idea what these creeps expect me to do. Where's that dog when I could use a hand?*

14

*A*s no surprise to Abby, Finlay did not appear in the cavern. Tavis eyed her impatiently and Mavis looked as if he might want to take a bite out of her. Tavis returned to his throne and smoothed his hair. "My dear, I sense you are stalling. Do you want to help our unjustly imprisoned brethren or not?"

Abby gulped as butterflies pounded against the walls of her stomach. "Of course I do," she said, making great effort to sound sincere. "It's just that..." Abby glanced at the cavern floor next to Mavis's throne. "May I..." Abby cleared her throat. "May I have my bag please, Sirs?"

Mavis bared his teeth and looked to his brother. Tavis flashed back and forth so fast, the next thing she knew, Abby was holding her bag and Tavis was sitting in his throne again stroking his chin. "No tricks," growled Mavis. Abby nodded in agreement and unzipped the side pouch of her backpack and pulled out her water bottle. The brothers both raised a suspicious eyebrow. Mavis rolled a ball of energy along his fingers as Abby chugged the last of her water. Wondering how she could stall further in hopes of figuring a way out, Abby returned the bottle to its place, zipped the pouch and shouldered her bag.

Tavis swooped his arm in a grand manner. "Proceed..."

Abby gulped audibly and began to panic. *Okay. Stay calm, stay calm, stay calm. These guys probably expect me to do some kind of magic spell. Maybe if I pretend to cast magic and they see it doesn't work, they'll realize I'm not 'the gifted one' and let me go.* Abby's stomach churned. *Or, perhaps Mavis will eat me.*

Abby smiled sheepishly at the brothers and turned away from them to focus on the nearest wall. *Here goes nothing!* Abby lifted her hands in the air and swirled them in a circle in front of her. She gracefully pulled her fingers back into fists, then dramatically flung her open hands forward toward the wall, yelling "Abracadabra!" Abby glanced over her shoulder nervously, half expecting Mavis to fry her with an orb.

Tavis motioned with his hand for her to continue. "You must cast your spell three times, as the prophecy says...the third of three...only then will our brethren be free."

Abby turned back to the wall, feeling weak in the knees. She raised her hands in front of her and repeated the same motions again. "Abracadabra!"

Tavis encouraged her from his throne. "Marvelous, my dear, once more and complete what you were meant to do."

A lump formed in Abby's throat. *Alright, this is it.* Images of her family flashed through Abby's mind. She choked back a tear and raised her hands in front of her, not caring this time if she followed the same motions. Abby squeezed her eyes tight and yelled out. "Abracadabra!!" When nothing happened, a rumbling hiss that shook the cavern emanated from what she knew must be Mavis. Abby slowly opened her eyes and turned to face her captors, expecting the worst.

Tavis shook his head in disappointment and extended an arm in front of Mavis when it appeared he may lunge at Abby. "What have I told you about such behavior, Brother?" Mavis growled, relaxing back into his throne.

Thinking fast, Abby blurted out, "I...I'm sincerely sorry, Sirs. I don't know why it didn't work." Tavis gave Abby a cold stare as she continued. "I think I must be exhausted from the journey here...perhaps if I rested for a while and had something to eat, I could try again later?"

Abby stood silent as Tavis continued to bear cold eyes upon her, all the while rubbing his chin. Mavis flashed his teeth at Abby and she was certain he would snap her head off were Tavis not present.

After what seemed like hours to Abby, Tavis quit rubbing his chin and flashed to tower over her. He wrapped his slender finger around her golden curl, twirling it silently. Abby fought her knocking knees until Tavis finally broke the silence. "Very well, my dear. You may rest, but know we are not finished here."

A wave of relief washed over Abby when it registered she had bought herself some time to figure a way out of the caves. Tavis released Abby's curl and motioned to Mavis. "Dear Brother, would you be so kind as to put our guest with the others?" Mavis growled but nodded briefly in affirmation as he zipped to Abby's side and took her by the arm. Mavis whisked Abby away from the center of the cavern, opposite the entrance they had used. A multitude of feelings rushed through Abby's body as they approached a tunnel she hadn't noticed before. Thankful to be alive, yet terrified of what lay ahead, it took a moment for Abby to realize what Tavis had said just moments ago. *Put our guest with the others?*

***

Mavis's grip on Abby's upper arm sizzled as he pulled her through a zigzagged, cramped tunnel. The glowing, green walls seemed to be closing in on them and Abby pondered where the path would lead. Examining her captor, Abby wondered how loyal Mavis was to his brother's demands; would he put her with 'the others' or finish her off in some deep, dark whole? Abby cleared her throat and spoke softly. "E-excuse me Mavis, Sir, but what exactly did your brother mean by putting me with 'the others'?"

Abby felt the grip around her arm tighten and burn momentarily. Mavis slowed the duo to a stop and towered over Abby, pushing her against the tunnel wall. With pointed teeth bared, saliva dripped from the corner of his mouth as he hissed. "Silence!" Mavis locked eyes with Abby. The deep, black pools of his irises seemed to tunnel into her. Her knees trembled and without saying a word, Abby nodded in affirmation. When Mavis seemed pleased with Abby's demeanor, he resumed whisking her through the long tunnel.

After several minutes, Abby gave up trying to memorize the twists and turns they took. She felt completely lost. *This is hopeless. How will I ever get home, let alone out of this mountain? Where is Rory? Where is Finlay? Have they figured out I'm missing? Will they even think I'm missing? Maybe they think I sneaked off to try to find my own way back home.*

As Abby continued to ponder her fate, the tunnel began to straighten out and open up into a small, dark chamber void of the faeries' magic. Mavis slowed to a stop and indicated for Abby to stand in the middle of the cave. Abby followed his request in silence, fearing what might happen next. Mavis crossed in front of her to a jagged wall. He waved his hand from left to right and muttered several words in an unintelligible language. Abby jumped back as the wall burst into a pulsating, green field. She peered forward and did a double take, realizing where once stood a jagged wall, there appeared to be a new tunnel.

Mavis turned back to Abby and pointed to the field. "Enter."

Abby gulped, terrified to do as he said and even more so not to. Mavis growled softly at her as he continued to point to, and beyond, the pulsing field. Abby decided that instance she would rather take her chances stepping into the energy and face whatever may lie beyond than stay there with Mavis one moment longer.

Taking a deep breath, Abby stood up straight and held her chin high as she stepped toward the wall. She secured her bag on her back and kept her eyes forward, ignoring the penetrating stare from Mavis. When she reached the glowing field, she paused and raised a cautionary hand in front of her. A familiar hiss sounded from behind. Abby knew she must be quick about it so she squeezed her eyes shut, held a deep breath and jumped forward through the field.

For a moment, Abby's entire body felt of pins and needles, but it didn't burn as she expected it to. When she opened her eyes, Abby patted her body to make sure she was in one piece. To her surprise, the field was gone, replaced by another jagged wall. And to her disappointment, she was swallowed by cold and darkness.

Abby stretched both arms out to her sides to feel for walls. Relieved, she found herself in what must be a tunnel with walls no more than three feet apart. Abby kept her hands on the cool surface and breathed deep. *You can do this. It can't be any worse than being alone with that faerie-devil. Just take slow steps and always keep a hand on the wall.*

After finishing her own pep talk, Abby strode forward carefully. To her relief, the tunnel wall was not jagged like the passage she entered through, but the cold was making her fingers numb. *I sure hope this leads somewhere soon.*

Abby traveled forward cautiously for several minutes, following the slow turn of the tunnel. She wasn't sure if it was her mind playing tricks, but Abby sensed the tunnel was no longer pitch black. She continued on for what seemed an eternity. The tunnel made a sudden, sharp left turn and opened into a gigantic cavern. Off in the distance, a green field that appeared to act as a barrier stretched from floor to ceiling. Abby's eyes were temporarily blinded from the intense glow. She stood still, palming the wall for support as her eyes adjusted to the light, and when they had, Abby gasped at what she saw. *Guess I've found the others!*

18

A bustling mini-village, it seemed, spread out before Abby. The area was dissected by a snaking, green stream that worked its way to the furthest end of the barrier and disappeared deep into the cavern wall. Abby gazed in amazement, and with a bit of disbelief, as she counted all the heads she could see. Twenty, perhaps. She stood in awe of what laid before her. Women of all ages went about their business. One appeared to be baking bread over a strange green fire, one was running a loom, one was stitching clothing, one was braiding the hair of another, a handful appeared to be playing a game, one was tending to several chickens, one pulled a net filled with fish from the stream, and one was headed straight toward her.

An aged woman, slight of build, announced over her shoulder to the group as she strode to Abby with purpose. "Those rotten brothers 'ave done it again, ladies." Abby heard a collective gasp and whisperings throughout the cave as faces turned to find her. The woman reached Abby's side and patted her on the shoulder. "There, there, Dearie, ye 'ave nothin' to worry 'bout now. Me name's Agatha and yer safe with us."

The woman took Abby's hand and directed her into the vast chamber toward the happenings. Abby was at a loss for words as she gazed around at all the faces; some beginning to wrinkle, some young and fresh. She gasped when she noticed they all had something in common, at least for those that she could see: a golden curl, if their hair was not already gray.

Abby stumbled and grasped Agatha's shoulder. "I, I need to sit down for a moment if you don't mind.

Agatha pointed to one of the younger girls. "Elli, be a dear and get the poor lassie a stool."

Abby smiled as Elli brought her a short stool with a deer skin covered seat. "Thank you, Elli." Abby swung her backpack to the ground and cringed inwardly as she was certain Elli couldn't be more than nine.

Agatha called out to another woman. "Violet, fetch some hot tea and bread for our newcomer. I reckon she's famished."

The woman called Violet was promptly at Abby's side with a wooden cup and a small loaf of bread. The aroma from the bread reminded Abby she was indeed ravenous and she accepted the offerings whole-heartedly. Abby glanced into the cup and raised a questioning brow upon seeing green liquid. "Is this safe to drink?"

Agatha chuckled in reply. "Aye, Lass. No need to worry. That's faerie magic at work, but it will do ye no harm."

Abby considered her need for food and drink, then shrugged as she tried the tea. Most of the captives stayed their distance and whispered to one another as Abby then tore into the bread. When she had finished, she handed the cup back to Violet. "Thank you all, that was very kind of you. I'm feeling a bit better now."

Agatha smiled warmly. "Of course, Dearie. Mary's tea always seems to have that effect."

Elli giggled at Abby and made a wiping motion across her lips. "Makes yer lips green, but only for a moment."

Abby groaned and wiped her face with the back of her hand as Agatha gently scolded Elli. "Quit yer teasing, Elli, the lass has enough to take in today."

Elli blushed and whispered an apology. "Sorry then."

Abby motioned to Agatha it was okay and shot a smile at the young girl. Abby then stood and surveyed the cavern again. The area was much larger than where she had been with Mavis and Tavis. The far right of the cave had a glowing field, just like the one Mavis had created, running from wall to wall, ceiling to ceiling, acting as a barrier to a smaller section of cave. There appeared to be several entrances to the chamber on the opposite side of the field. *Hmm. I suppose that field will zap you. No one is on the opposite side of it, so I guess everyone is trapped in here.*

Agatha placed a gentle hand on Abby's arm. "And what shall we call ye by?"

Abby pulled away from her thoughts. "Oh...ah...my name's Abby." A million questions were now forming in Abby's head as she continued to examine her surroundings. "Agatha, did all of you come here through that tunnel I came out of?"

Agatha nodded. "Aye, that we did Abby."

Abby pondered the answer quietly.

The older woman smiled warmly again. "Ye ask as

many questions as ye like, Abby."

Abby sat down on the stool again. As she did, Agatha, Violet, and Elli pulled similar stools into a circle with Abby. "How did everyone come to be here?" Abby paused, looking for better words. "What I mean is, was everyone kidnapped? I was brought here by two, filthy thieves."

All three of Abby's new companions nodded in unison. Elli interjected with fervor. "I had a sack pulled over me head when I went to fetch water for me mum."

Violet agreed quietly. "Aye, many of us were brought to this ominous place by the pair of them dreadful men. They hunt the countryside for those wicked faeries. Seems the brothers can't leave the mountain so they make those men do their nasty deeds for 'em."

Abby questioned, already knowing the answer. "You mean Mavis and Tavis, right?"

Agatha nodded. "Aye. But some of the girls were brought here by a ferocious, green beast. Consider ye'self lucky to only have encountered those thieves."

Abby frowned at Agatha's words. *Ferocious, green beast...surely she doesn't mean Finlay.* "So was everyone brought here forced to try to free all the faeries stuck in the walls? Tavis told me I must fulfill some prophecy, that I was the gifted one."

Violet rolled her eyes. "He says that to everyone. Don't be fooled by his charm."

"An' they're obsessed with ar' hair," piped Elli, "if ye hadn't noticed, we all have, or had," she said, pointing to several grey haired women, "a golden curl in ar' hair."

Violet snorted. "Aye. Tavis indeed likes to go on about some golden drop."

Abby nodded. "Yes, I did hear all about that." *And read all about it. I wonder if they know about the prophecy on the scroll I found.* Abby sat in silence considering the situation.

After studying Abby's seemingly confused face, Agatha questioned, "What are yer thoughts, Abby?"

"Well," Abby paused and scratched her chin. "My biggest question at this moment is why do the faeries keep everyone locked up in here? I mean, I'm assuming you can't pass through that green field, right? Why keep everyone here? It's obvious to me that Mavis and Tavis are not the good-fairing creatures I always imagined faeries to be. Why didn't they kill each of us when we failed to perform?"

Agatha sighed. "Dearest Abby, the answer to yer question lies in the brother's obsession with Enya Myst. I'm certain ye heard all about her?"

Abby nodded. "Yes, I did. But Tavis said that Enya was obsessed with them. So it was the other way around?"

"Aye," replied Agatha. "Those faerie brothers worshiped that girl. Enya was a beauty like no other, and with a heart to match. She didn't take kindly to violence or hatred of any type. In hopes of gaining her favor, Mavis and Tavis pledged to her they would never take the life of another."

Abby blurted, "But I thought they killed the Red King?"

"It's true." Agatha nodded in surprise at Abby's knowledge. "When Enya learned of what the faeries had done, she was beside herself at the loss of her one true love. It was then her faither cast a powerful spell upon the faeries. We all wish he had brought them to their end, but he honored Enya's wishes not to kill them. Instead, he locked them up for eternity, all but Mavis and Tavis who managed to escape somehow."

Abby took a guess at finishing the story. "So, I suppose because Mavis and Tavis are nuts and still worship this Enya, who I'm guessing must have died long ago, they won't kill anyone that's brought here? Instead, they leave you – well, I guess us now – locked up. And I bet they don't let anyone go free because they don't want to be found out!"

"There ye have it, Abby," confirmed Agatha as she shifted on her stool.

Looking at the stools brought another question to Abby's mind. "Agatha? Where did you get all the things you have here? How on earth are any of you able to survive?"

Agatha snorted. "Those filthy thieves bring us just enough to get by, per the bidding of their 'Masters'." Standing, Agatha beckoned for Abby to follow. "Enough of this talk for now, there will be plenty o' time for figurin' things out. Let me show ye around yer new home."

Abby's heart sank at the thought of being trapped in the cave for the rest of her life. *Surely Finlay or Rory will come looking for me.* Abby followed Agatha throughout the cavern, taking in all the faces and names. She was greeted with smiles and hugs and was surprised by how happy all of the women and girls seemed, all except one. Across one of several, small footbridges spanning the stream, a lone woman sat in the shadows of the cavern, her knees pulled tight to her chest as she rocked back and forth, humming a sad tune to herself.

"Agatha?" Abby tapped her escort on the shoulder. "What's the matter with her? She looks so sad."

Agatha frowned. "That poor soul is Victoria. She's forever mourning the loss of her children. We've tried everythin' to sooth her but to no avail." Agatha approached Victoria and rubbed her back. "There, there dear friend, come an' say hello to our newest sister."

Victoria slowly rose and straightened her worn dress. She accepted a stable hand from Agatha as they stepped into the flickers of a nearby green-glowing pit that seemed to serve as a fire. She gazed around the cavern and eventually locked eyes with Abby. Abby smiled and said hello after several awkwardly silent moments passed. The air remained still and Abby began to wonder if Victoria could even speak. A range of emotions seemed to wash over the woman's face as she continued to stare at Abby. Abby smiled nervously not knowing if she should say something else to this strange person.

Agatha gave Victoria a gentle squeeze on the arm. "Well don't be rude, say hello."

Victoria breathed deeply and whispered only one word. "Sage?"

***

Abby's stomach lurched into her throat as she struggled to make sense of what this peculiar woman just said to her. Abby studied Victoria's face until it dawned on her she was looking at an aged version of herself and her sister. *It can't be.*

Abby questioned suspiciously, yet as politely as she could manage. "How-how do you know that name?"

Tears began to well in Victoria's eyes as she stepped toward Abby. "Sa-Sage. Is it really you?"

Abby took an uncertain step back. "Sage is my sister. How do you know that name?"

Victoria gasped violently causing the bustle of the cavern to go silent. A new range of emotions flooded her face as she exclaimed, "Abigail, my baby?" Victoria outstretched her arms toward Abby and began to hum a sweet melody.

Fragmented memories sprung from Abby's past, whirling through her mind as she listened to the tune. Only one person called her by her birth name, and that person was taken from her many years ago. Abby attempted to keep a distance between herself and Victoria as she struggled to make sense of what was happening, but her mother inched closer and closer, humming her sweet tune louder with every step. As Victoria wrapped her arms around her daughter, a sudden realization flooded through Abby that not only was she was no longer alone, her mother was indeed alive. The tough exterior Abby fought to uphold for many days prior burst into a sea of tears. "Mom, we all thought you were dead."

***

Abby and her mother sat next to one of the green fires for hours getting to know one another. Victoria crept from her sullen shell and with a beaming face, she eagerly asked Abby every question she could think of. "And what of my dear Jonathon?" Victoria asked cautiously. "Did he remarry? I wouldn't blame him if he did."

Abby shook her head immediately. "No way, Mom. You were the love of his life; he hasn't even had a girlfriend since you've been gone, not even when we were in the States."

"You were in the States? Why?" Victoria's face lit up as she continued. "Oh! Did they still have one of those corner coffee shops I loved so? I think it was called Star-bursts."

Abby snorted at her latter question. "Yeah, Mom, something like that. They had plenty of those, trust me. Dad would make a point to stop there when we took trips into town. I guess that makes sense now. I'm sure it reminded him of you." Abby paused as she thought back to her childhood. "He was so distraught over your, ah, 'death', I think he needed to get away from Scotland for a while. We moved to his grandfather's farm in Nebraska. I think we were there for at least a decade, but then Dad started going on and on about this special book he had to find. He was obsessed over it, said it would change our lives. He thought it was hidden somewhere in Scotland, so he moved us back to Kinloch-Rannoch."

Victoria stared down at her folded hands. "All the pain I've caused..."

Seeing a hint of sadness return to her mother's face, Abby redirected the conversation and asked some questions of her own. "Mom, I still don't understand how you got here. Do you really not remember a thing of that day?"

Victoria stared into the pulsing green pit, deep in thought. "Well," she started slowly, "I remember I was exploring the mountainside near home. I think, I think I was investigating a well."

Abby nodded. "The Well of Fair Maidens."

Victoria raised a finger as she repeated the name questionably. "The Well of Fair Maidens? Why, yes! That sounds familiar to me." Abby's mother gasped and caught her breath. "My book! I remember reading about that in my book!"

Abby thought back to her last visit to her father's shop. "You mean *The Peoples of Faerie Mountain*?"

Victoria looked surprised. "Yes! You've seen my book?"

Abby answered hesitantly, unsure if she should break the trust of Mrs. MacTavish. "Oh. Well, I came across it in Dad's book store one day, when I was helping straighten things up in the back."

Victoria appeared lost in thought again as she began to hum a soft melody. Curling a strand of Abby's hair around her finger, she began to recall the day of her disappearance. "I remember I was curious about the creatures in the book. I just had to know if they truly existed. Nothing would stop me that day." Victoria paused and smiled thoughtfully. "I was quite stubborn back then, I refused to heed the warnings of your father. He said he had a bad feeling and didn't want me poking around the mountainside by myself."

Abby mimicked her mother's action and wrapped a now grayed curl of her elder around her own finger. "So let me guess...you sneaked off without telling anyone?"

Victoria lowered her eyes and nodded. "It was so silly of me. It cost me, well us, everything."

Abby stroked her mother's hand. "It's okay Mom. You

couldn't have known." Abby choked back a snort. "And believe me...the stubbornness runs in the family!"

Abby's mom chuckled as if out of practice. "Is that so? I'll have to remember that young lady!"

Abby blushed and changed the subject. "So what happened when you got to the mountain? Did you find the faeries?"

Victoria shook her head. "Quite the contrary, I found nothing but an old, dried up well. I sat for a while daydreaming of what life must of been like when it was a working well." Victoria stared into the fire again, searching her memories. "I guess I must have lost track of time and awareness of my surroundings. A terrible storm rolled in. One moment I was basking in the rays of the sun and the next I was struggling to right myself against the wind and rain."

Abby squeezed her mother's hand, coaxing her to continue. "Did you fall into the well, Mom?"

A puzzled look spread across Victoria's face. "I...well, I'm not entirely sure. Things are a bit fuzzy at that point. I remember a powerful gust of wind bowling me over. I think I must have hit my head on the well, but I also had a sense of falling and then..."

"And then what?" Abby asked eagerly.

Victoria sat quiet for several moments. "This will probably sound strange, but when I felt like I was falling, something warm and soft enveloped me. I seemed to sense a faint green glow around the edges of the blackness that wrapped around me. And then, I was here. Well, not here, but in another part of the cave and those wicked brothers towered over me. And I guess you must know the rest."

Abby sat quite as her body began to quiver. *Something warm and soft. A green glow. It can't be so. Finlay stole my mom!*

16

*A*bby continued to quiver as she worked to calm herself. Her mother eyed her quizzically and began to question Abby's sudden change in demeanor. "Abigail, what on earth is the matter?"

Abby opened her mouth to respond but was distracted by a faint and unusual sound behind her. Abby raised a pausing finger toward her mother as she twisted her torso in the direction of the continuing noise. "Psstt." Abby craned her neck further trying to key in on the sound. "Psssttt." Abby finally realized the nearly inaudible noise was coming from just beyond the glowing wall. "Psstt. A-by." Abby froze momentarily in disbelief before jumping up, crossing the footbridge, and running to where the green force field met the far edge of the cavern wall. "Rory!" Abby stopped short of the buzzing wall, her heart pounding. "Rory, what are you doing here?"

Rory was crouched behind a larger boulder, unsure of his surroundings. He spoke soft yet firm. "I should ask ye the same thing! Why did ye sneak off, A-by?"

Abby frowned. "I'm sorry Rory. I wanted to investigate the well. I thought...I don't know what I thought I would find, but it brought me a bucket of trouble. Those two greasy thieves grabbed me and brought me here!"

Rory continued to whisper. "Ye are fortunate I spied

yer thieves creeping from a crevice in the mountainside. I searched for ye for hours an' when I saw them, I knew somethin' was amiss."

Abby crept as close as she could to the prison wall. Her face tingled as she leaned in. "Rory, we have to figure out how to get rid of this magic monstrosity. Those faerie brothers you didn't think existed, Mavis and Tavis....well, they're real and they're here! They're trying to break a spell that's keeping the rest of their kind imprisoned in the cave walls." Abby glanced around, afraid someone would notice Rory. "They think a girl with a golden curl in her hair has the power to free the faeries. And they apparently know about the prophecy on my scroll. All these people are being held against their will when they are unable to perform. We have to do something, and fast!"

Rory stood to examine the green field. He scrunched his face as he considered the gravity of the problem. "Perhaps it's an illusion." He raised a hand and moved to touch the buzzing wall.

"Rory, don't!" Abby exclaimed. "It might burn you."

Rory paused momentarily at Abby's protest. He then skimmed his hand along the surface of the wall with no apparent effect.

Abby thought back to the glowing field Mavis forced her to walk through in the not so distant past. As she began to give Rory a second warning, he strode through the wall and stood next to her. He examined his body for injury and once satisfied, grinned from ear to ear. "See, it's just a fancy trick."

Abby groaned and shook her head. "Rory, I was about to tell you I'm pretty sure it's one way. You can get in but you can't get out."

Rory grunted in disbelief and reached a hand toward the field again. As his fingers neared the glowing wall, a green tendril spurted out and zapped his wrist. Rory quickly pulled his hand back.

"Aye. It appears I acted with haste. I should have listened to ye, A-by."

Abby sighed. "There's nothing to be done about it now, is there? We just need to find a way out of here." Abby scratched her head as she examined the cave wall. *I wonder if there's some type of hidden switch to shut this field down. But if there were, wouldn't someone have discovered it by now?* Abby continued to ponder the problem, unaware of the audience she and her companion were drawing.

Victoria placed a hand on her daughter's shoulder to get her attention. "Abigail, what's going on here? Who is this young man and where did he come from?" Just as Abby was turning in response, she heard excited whisperings all around. Agatha weaved her way to the front of the gathering crowd and gaped when she saw Rory.

Butterflies began dancing in Abby's stomach. "What's the matter Agatha? You look like you've seen a ghost."

Agatha dabbed her forehead with a worn kerchief. "I believe I have, Lassie." Steadying herself, she motioned toward Rory. "Because that there is the Red King!"

***

Agatha attempted to regain her composure as Rory

rolled his eyes and whispered in Abby's ear. "How long have these people been locked away, A-by? I think she's gone mad."

Whispering back, Abby gave Rory a swift poke in the ribs. "That's not funny, Rory." Abby continued as Rory grimaced and rubbed his side. "I for one would like to hear what Agatha has to say."

Abby motioned for Agatha to step closer. "Agatha, this is my, ah, friend, Rory. Why did you say he is the Red King?"

Agatha rubbed her chin for a moment as she examined the young man before her. "I don't believe me eyes," she said, dabbing her forehead again. "When I was a wee one, I saw our great protector of the countryside with me own eyes. Wasn't long after the wickedness took him."

Abby frowned and touched Agatha's arm. "So you were taken from your family as a child..." Abby paused to scratch her head. "That was over two hundred years ago...shouldn't you be dead?"

"No child. That creature musta brought me forward in time, the best I can tell. But regardless, I saw the passing of many cold spells after the Red King was slain. Me hair was just beginnin' to go grey when that despicable, green beast brought me here. I was the first one, ye see...don't know how long it's been, but many, many moons, I suppose," Agatha paused and looked to Rory again. "But no' too many moons to know the Red King when I see him!"

Rory stepped forward and gently cleared his throat. "Beg yer pardon, Agatha, but I've lived no more than 16 years. It's no' reasonable to believe I'm the Red King."

Agatha flapped her kerchief in the air, seemingly oblivious to Rory's words. She continued to examine him head to toe and circled him slowly. Agatha stopped behind him and gasped when she saw his sword. "Yer sword, may I see it?"

Rory groaned and turned to face Agatha. He carefully pulled the sword from the makeshift scabbard across his back and held it out for the insistent woman to see.

Agatha held her breath as she ran her fingers over the hilt, then cautiously over the intricate symbols on the blade. Slowly exhaling, Agatha whispered, "It's a powerful and mighty sword...can free us all from this nightmare."

Rory grunted with frustration and returned the sword to its place along his back. "I don't know what to say. I am no' the Red King and me sword is just that. A sword."

Abby put herself between Agatha and her companion. "Perhaps we should give Rory a little space and continue this discussion later. I imagine he could use a serving of that special tea and some bread."

Looking discouraged, Agatha was silent for a moment then nodded her head in agreement. "Aye, I suppose ye're right. After all, there'll be plenty o' time to talk some sense into yer friend." Agatha called into the gathered crowd. "Elli, could ye fetch this lad some bread and tea?"

In a flash, Elli weaved her way to stand before Rory with the requested items. With a deep curtsy, she extended the offerings to Rory. "Here ye are, Sir." Elli blushed and looked at the ground as Rory accepted the food and drink.

Rory took pause when he saw the tea. Abby giggled

knowingly. "Don't worry, Rory, the tea is quite good."

"But why is it green, A-by?"

"Faerie magic. It's colored the tea, just like everything else in here. It won't hurt you."

Rory shrugged and smiled as he indulged. After shoving the last bite into his mouth and handing the cup back to Elli, he mumbled, "It's quite kind. I thank thee."

Elli backed away and tugged on Agatha's sleeve. She whispered shyly as she glanced at the red-headed stranger. "Was wondering something."

Agatha smiled and stroked Elli's hair. "What's on yer mind, lassie?"

"If Sir here is the Red King, what will happen if the wicked faeries come to check on us like they sometimes do?"

Abby slapped a hand to her head. "Ah geez! I didn't even think about that." Abby glanced nervously outside of the glowing wall. "Do they come in here often?"

"Aye, they do," replied Agatha, "and I imagine they ar' due for a visit any time now."

Abby frowned and put her hands on her hips. "Well, if Rory really looks as much like the Red King as you say, we need to hide him." Abby scanned the prison. "But where?"

Elli tugged purposefully on Agatha's sleeve again. "He could put a dress on, an' cover his head."

Rory threw his hands in front of him. "No. I will no' wear a dress. Let these foul creatures come and see me. I will give them a fight if that is what they seek!"

Abby grabbed Rory by the wrists. "Rory, they're right. We need to hide you! You have no idea what Mavis and Tavis are capable of." Rory stood silent, passing a stubborn glare to Abby. "Please, Rory, I've seen the magic these creeps possess. I don't want you to get hurt, or worse."

Rory gave in and relaxed his shoulders with a sigh. "Aye, A-by. If it will please ye, do what ye must."

***

Several of the women directed Rory toward the furthermost depths of the chamber and began bustling about. One crudely measured his stature with a piece of rope while the others carefully removed the sword from his back, then went about grabbing various, drab garments. Abby settled in by the green pit once again with Victoria and giggled as Rory made theatrical faces at her. In the end, it was decided to simply pull a dress over Rory's existing clothes and wrap a shawl around his head. Rory carried his sword to the pit and eased himself to the ground next to Abby.

Abby snorted and smiled mischievously at Rory. "That color's good on you. And the embroidered flower really brings out your eyes."

Rory returned the smile and comically batted his eyelashes, sending Abby into a fit of laughter. Once Abby had composed herself, she put on a serious face and motioned to her mom. "Rory, I want to introduce you to someone. This will no doubt surprise you, but this is my mom, Victoria."

Rory stared at Victoria quizzically as she reached around the pit and extended a hand to him. With the utmost care, Rory gave her hand a squeeze and said, "It's an honor." With a confused look, he turned back to Abby. "I don't understand, A-by. How can that be? Ye said yer mither died when you were a wee one."

"It's a long story, Rory, and I don't have all the details, but it appears Finlay kidnapped her, as well as some of the others here in the cave."

Fiery anger flashed across Rory's face. "I knew that beast was no' what he seemed. He can't be trusted, A-by!"

Abby frowned and sighed. "I need to talk to him first before I jump to any conclusions. I remember him telling me once he was bound by faerie magic and had to do their bidding. But we all deserve to know why he didn't refuse to do such horrible things...ripping people away from their loved ones and putting them in danger." Abby choked on her words as she stared into her mother's eyes. "Just look at what he did to you..."

Victoria took Abby's hand in her own. "We cannot change the past, my sweet. Do not let the hatred seething from those beastly faerie brothers envelope your heart. We must focus on the future. Surely we will find our way home, back to your dear father and sister. I can feel it in my bones." Victoria closed her eyes and began to hum a soothing tune. Abby sat in silence and allowed the sweet melody to wrap around her. As she soaked in the warmth of the fire and her mother's lullaby, Abby noticed Rory staring at her mother with an odd look on his face. Victoria continued to hum as Abby released her hand and scooted around the fire to Rory.

"Rory, what is it? What's wrong? Why are you looking at my mom like that?" Rory continued staring at Victoria in silence, mesmerized by the song in the air. Abby gave him a gentle shake on the shoulder. "Hey, Numpty, snap out of it."

Rory blinked his eyes rapidly and directed his attention to Abby. "I...I know that song, A-by."

Abby scrunched her face in surprise. "Really? Are you sure about that, Rory? I've never heard it before. It doesn't sound like anything on the radio."

Rory nodded emphatically. "Me mither used to hum it to me when I was just a wee lad. I guess it took me back to that place for a moment."

Abby shrugged. "Hmm. Interesting." Abby shifted toward her mom. "Hey, Mom?"

Victoria abruptly opened her eyes and quit humming. "Yes, my little one?"

"Mom, do you remember where you learned that song?"

Victoria contemplated the question as she stared into the pit. "I'm quite certain it was from Mrs. MacTavish. Why do you ask, dear?"

"Well, Rory says..." Abby paused as Agatha pulled a squat stool to the fire.

"Pardon me for interruptin', but it's time the Red King and I had a talk!"

17

*R*ory scowled at the words directed toward him. "I don't know why ye keep insisting such a foolish thing. I am Rory MacKay of the Clan MacKay. I 'ave lived me life by the waters of Loch Black, no' roamin' the countryside battlin' faeries of long ago."

Agatha smiled at Rory's response. "There, there, young lad. No need to get ye so worked up." Agatha pointed to Rory's sword. "How did ye come across such a fine weapon?"

Rory calmed himself before answering the question. "From me faither."

Agatha nodded. "I see, and do ye know where ye faither got it?"

Rory responded hesitantly. "Me faither once said it was passed to him by his faither and he would one day do the same with me." Rory looked to the ground. "I was no' ready to receive it though."

Abby reached out and traced the symbols on the hilt of the sword. "You miss him dearly, don't you?"

Rory continued to stare at the ground. "Aye, A-by."

Agatha empathetically touched Rory on the shoulder. "Rory, do ye think it's a fair statement to say this sword has been in yer family for a long, long time then?"

Rory looked into the pit thoughtfully and after a moment turned to meet Agatha's eyes. "Aye, Agatha...would be a fair statement. I don't know its origins though, only it was passed from faither to son many times."

Agatha patted Rory on the hand. "As much as ye don't want to believe it, I've laid eyes on this very sword before; it's the only one like it." Rory grunted as Agatha continued. "While ye may no' be 'the' Red King, there's no doubt in me mind that ye carry his blood in yer veins."

Rory shook his head. "I dunno, me faither never mentioned such a thing."

Abby reached inside the shawl encompassing Rory's fiery braids and gave one a gentle tug. "Rory, I think what Agatha is saying isn't so far-fetched. I'm sure you remember me telling you I've seen that symbol on your sword before, and it was always in conjunction with the Red King. Why is it so hard for you to believe you could be his descendant?"

Rory continued to shake his head as Agatha shocked Abby with her words. "The Prophecy of Myst says the Red King will come again."

Abby's eyes popped wide. "Whoa, what did you just say?!"

Agatha repeated herself slowly. "The Prophecy of Myst tells of a rightful warrior; a true, just soul regaining the power. Me gut tells me he's sittin' before us."

Abby squeezed Rory's arm and whispered in his ear. "The scroll! That sounds like part of the prophecy you translated for me!" Abby scrambled up to grab her backpack. She eagerly plopped back down by the pit and rummaged through a pouch until her hands wrapped around the growingly familiar leather roll. "A-ha!" Abby pulled the scroll from her bag, then retrieved the small notepad she used to write the English translation.

Agatha scooted her stool around the pit to sit next to Abby. "What 'ave ye got there, Abby?"

Abby handed the scroll to Agatha. "I wasn't sure I should say anything, but you obviously know something about this."

Agatha sucked in a slow breath as she carefully took the scroll from Abby and unrolled it. "Oh me! Lassie! It's the scroll of Myst. It was written by the beautiful Enya after the death of her faither." Agatha exhaled and whispered with amazement. "Where did ye find it?"

"Well," Abby said, "I was searching a small cave somewhere in this mountain, but it was in 'my' time. It was hidden in a secret cubby in the back of the cave. I tucked it in my backpack just before..." Abby trailed off, uncertain if she should say anymore.

"What is it, Lassie?" Agatha encouraged.

Abby looked to her mom, Rory, then Agatha before answering. "Here's the thing. I've recently had several encounters with a magical dog, the one many here, including yourself, Agatha, refer to as a beast."

Agatha rubbed Abby on the knee soothingly. "It's a shame, Lassie. I'm so sorry ye had to experience that."

Abby shook her head. "There's nothing to be sorry about. He never hurt me, in fact, up until now, I've actually felt safe with him and even trusted him."

Agatha scrunched her face at the thought. "Felt safe with him? What exactly do ye mean?"

"Well," Abby hesitated, "there's more to it than you might believe..."

Agatha made a hurried motion with her hands. "On with it then."

"Alright, I'm just going to lay it all out there. The short of it is I can communicate with said beast."

"Pppffhh!" Agatha raised an eyebrow.

Trying not to get discouraged, Abby continued. "No! Really! His name is Finlay and he brought me here to find the Red King. He says the Red King must set him free. Finlay is bound by the faerie's magic...I guess he has to do whatever they tell him to."

Agatha stared at the scroll and contemplated Abby's words. "Hmm, if this is so, seems there may be hidden things at play." Agatha raised another eyebrow to Abby. "How exactly is it ye can communicate with this creature?"

Abby tingled with excitement, eager to explain. "I can hear him in my head. And if I just think the words, he can hear me in reply. Where I come from, I think it's called telepathy."

Agatha nodded, "I see, I see. Had I no' been through what I'd been through, I would think ye mad."

Rory interjected, "I didn't believe it at first either, but the dog knew things that convinced me."

"Let me ask ye this, Lassie," Agatha questioned, pointing to Rory, "How exactly did ye find yer friend here?"

Abby thought back to her first encounter with Rory and smiled. "When Finlay brought me back in time, I landed smack on top of Rory on the mountainside." Abby paused as a thought struck her. "Now that I think about it, and knowing what I know now, it was no accident I ran into Rory."

Rory snorted at the memory. "Ye broke me bowe!"

Abby rolled her eyes. "That was an accident, Numpty. But seriously, Rory, consider it for a minute. If you could just believe for a moment what Agatha has said about you is correct, then wouldn't you agree it was no coincidence we met?" Abby continued before giving Rory a chance to reply. "I think Finlay has known about you all along."

"If this is so, Lassie," Agatha said while scratching her temple, "then why didn't the beast himself tell the young lad here to free him?"

Abby considered the question thoughtfully. "Well, for one, I don't think anyone else can communicate with him, but I remember asking Finlay why he didn't just find the Red King himself. He said it would mean his death, whatever that's supposed to mean."

Agatha gasped and jumped up from her stool and pointed beyond the glowing barrier just as several of the girls scattered throughout the cavern, shrieking in unison. "I'd say ye should ask him yerself, Lassie."

Abby jumped to her feet and followed the line of Agatha's gesture to find Finlay standing on the other side of the prison wall.

***

Abby ran to the shrieking girls now huddled in the center of the cave as Agatha followed behind. "Hey. It's okay! You guys don't have to be afraid of the dog. He's not going to hurt you." The girls quieted but continued to huddle as Agatha tried to calm them. Abby glanced over her shoulder to see Finlay pacing back and forth outside the barrier. Looking back to the girls, she said, "I promise it will be okay. Trust me. I'll take care of that fur-ball!" The group relaxed as Abby turned and stomped her way across a footbridge toward the buzzing, green field.

Abby strode within inches of the barrier and called out as loud as she could in her mind. *Hey!* Finlay swung his head toward the barricade and moved with smooth, calculated steps to stand just opposite Abby. Abby slapped her hands to her hips. *Where have you been? And what are you doing here?*

Finlay snorted and entered Abby's mind. *I've been searching for you and the boy.*

Well, you found us. I could have used your help earlier. I thought I was a goner.

Finlay cocked his head to the side and eyed Abby. *You appear to be in one piece to me, but I sense a level of stress and anger in your mind.*

Abby stamped her foot. *Of course I'm stressed and angry! I was kidnapped by those filthy thieves, forced to perform a ridiculous ceremony, thrown into a prison, and then Rory gets himself trapped too!*

Abby let out a deep breath in attempt to calm her shaking hands. *To top it all off, just when I was starting to really believe in you, I find out you've been kidnapping people and bringing them here where they are terrorized and imprisoned by your 'Masters'. And the worst of it...were you aware you brought my mother here thirteen years ago?!*

Finlay took a step back and shook his entire body as if he had just been doused with ice-cold water. Abby felt a sense of remorse overwhelm her mind. Finlay looked from Abby to each and every face in the chamber and in a gruff yet soothing voice replied, *I did not know, young one. Bring her to your side.*

Abby eyed Finlay suspiciously but decided there was no harm and waved her mother over to the barrier.

Just before reaching Abby's side, Victoria paused hesitantly, unsure of the strange dog in front of her. "What's going on, my dear Abigail?"

Abby brushed her mother's hand with her own. "It's okay, Mom. This is Finlay, the dog I was talking about. He's the one who brought you here. He just asked for you to join me, but I'm not sure why."

Finlay bowed his head as Victoria approached the field. *Please tell your mother I am honored to make her proper acquaintance.* Finlay swayed his head from side to side. *And I am eternally sorry to have taken her from you and your family so long ago.*

"Mom, Finlay wants me to tell you he's sorry for what he did."

Victoria stood silent as she soaked in Abby's words.

Abby turned her attention back to Finlay. *If you are eternally sorry, why'd you do it in the first place?*

Abby tapped her foot impatiently as Finlay hesitated. *Well?*

Finlay pawed the ground in front of him. He circled several times and then laid his body down with a thump. *Join me, little one.*

Abby raised an eyebrow and shrugged as she lowered herself to the ground and folded her legs. She motioned for her mother to do the same. *This better be good fur-face.*

Finlay grumbled as he entered Abby's mind. Intense imagery danced through her brain as he began to speak. *I remember the day clearly. The faeries had released me from the cave as normal to search for another possible key, as they call it. I felt an intense pull in time that drew me to your mother. It was unusual, I normally search for weeks or months until I find someone that fits the description. I had never felt a pull as such. I watched your mother on the mountainside for many hours. I was fascinated by her singing and dancing around an unkempt well. Her voice captivated me, but I knew if I ventured too close to her, as with the others, I would not be able to stop the faerie magic.*

Abby blinked and shook her head as she watched a younger version of her mother dance without inhibition around the Well of Fair Maidens. *What do you mean, Finlay, you wouldn't be able to stop the magic? What happens?*

Finlay considered his words before replying. *If my Masters have released me for the purpose of bringing another victim to them, they have the power to sense when I am engaged with someone and pull me, and 'their key', back to the cave, regardless of where, or when, I am. Nor can I resist their command to seek out the bearer of the power they so desperately desire. I do not understand their capabilities, but as you might say, I am their puppet.*

Abby cocked her head to one side and brushed a stray curl from her face. *So, what you are saying is you essentially have no choice in the matter?*

Finlay snorted and nodded his head. *That is correct, Lass.*

Abby leaned closer to the buzzing barrier. *What*

happened with my mom then?

A freak storm rolled across the mountainside. Rain began to fall in sheets, and the wind...I have never felt such force. Your mother leaned against the well for support but I sensed she was in trouble. She was thrown off balance by the wind and started to fall backwards into the well. I acted instinctively and crossed the distance between us just as she hit her head. As soon as I touched her, that was it, we were summoned back to the cave. I wanted to spare her, but it was beyond my control. Do you understand now, child?

Abby stared through the field into the deep pools of Finlay's eyes. Trusting her gut, Abby replied, *I forgive you, Finlay. I understand how you had no control in my mother's case, but why haven't you simply refused to bring others?*

Finlay lifted his head level with Abby's. *If I resist in any manner, the faeries will take my life. And if they take my life, I have no doubt they would find another means to their end.*

Abby furrowed her brow. *How does it ever end then? We have to stop them! If they find 'the key' they are after, I have a feeling bad things will happen.*

Finlay slowly stood and shook his body again, the magic binding him sizzled with the movement. *This is why the Red King must free me. Only then will all be set right.*

Abby jumped up and smoothed her hair. *Finlay, it was no accident you dropped me on top of Rory, was it?*

Finlay bowed his head. *No, Lass, it was not.*

He carries the blood line of the Red King, doesn't he?

Aye, Lass, that is so.

But you couldn't tell me because you'd be interfering.

And if Mavis and Tavis found out, they'd kill you on the spot. You had to trust I would figure it out on my own.

Finlay bowed his head again. *That is correct.*

Abby frowned. *We have a problem, other than the obvious. Rory doesn't believe he's related to the Red King. Even with the sword, and everything we've told him. He's pretty stubborn. I'm not sure what to do.*

Finlay tilted his head in thought. *Utilize those around you, Lass. There is one among you that bears the knowledge you need.*

How do you know that?

She is from the Red King's time.

Abby jumped up. *Of course, Agatha!*

18

*A*bby grabbed her mother's hand and pulled her across the closest bridge and back to the pit as she waved for Agatha to join them. Rory fiddled with the shawl over his head as Abby, Agatha, and Victoria settled in around the warmth. Abby swatted at Rory's hand. "Rory! Leave it alone. It's important for you to stay hidden; there's no telling when 'scary and scarier' might show up." Rory moaned but heeded Abby's warning.

Agatha nervously eyed Finlay as he paced back and forth outside the barrier. "Tell me, Lass, what did the beast 'ave to say for himself?"

Abby sighed. "I can only imagine what it's been like for you, and the others, trapped in here all these years. I don't expect this to make you feel any better, but Finlay basically had no choice in his actions. Mavis and Tavis have their magic wrapped up tight around him from what I gather. He didn't want to bring any of you here, and I know in my heart he's sorry. I can feel the remorse he bears."

Agatha considered Abby's words. "Well, he can make it up to us by gettin' us out of here!"

Abby frowned. "Yeah, there's the problem. I'm guessing Finlay can't just zip on in here and zip on out with anyone. I'm willing to bet there's more to that barrier than what we can see."

Abby flinched as Finlay unexpectedly entered her mind. *You are a smart one, Lass. What you say is correct. Were I to attempt to cross the field in any manner, the result would not be favorable.*

Abby cringed. *Well, I've never heard of fried dog and I really don't want to see one first hand.*

Abby jerked a thumb toward Finlay. "He says I'm right. He'd probably die if he tried to pass through it. So, we're going to have to figure out something else."

Agatha unrolled the scroll again and stared blankly at the writing. "Can anyone read this?"

Abby excitedly grabbed her notepad. "Rory translated it to English for me. I'll read it out loud for everyone. Maybe collectively, we can crack the code."

Clearing her throat, Abby immersed herself in the words.

> Green tendrils reign
> Engulf the land
> A rightful warrior
> Will come again.
> Heart and hand
> Head of fire
> A just, true soul
> Regains the power.
> A golden drop
> The third of three
> Bears the power
> To set them free.
> Fools beware

Rethink your hate

'Ere fire binds gold

To seal your fate.

As the last phrase escaped her mouth, Abby looked up to find the small group deep in thought. She cleared her throat again to pull everyone back to the moment. Agatha dabbed her forehead with her kerchief. "I've niver heard the whole thing before, only bits an' pieces. It's powerful words, me think, if ye know their true meaning."

Abby chortled, "No kidding. But I think half of this prophecy is clear now. The green tendril bit is obviously referring to faerie magic." Abby paused and turned to Rory. "And the reference to a rightful warrior coming again must mean a descendant of the Red King will regain the power."

Rory frowned and stared into the green pit. "I don't feel any 'power', A-by. It can't be so."

Victoria cut in and directed a verse toward Rory. "A just, true soul regains the power." Smiling as the thought came to her, she continued, "If you don't believe, young man, it will not be so."

Agatha nodded in agreement. "Listen to Victoria, Lad. She's a wise, wise woman. Search ye soul and perhaps ye shall find the truth."

Rory replied with his typical grunt and looked from his sword to the fire and back, lost in thought.

"Agatha," Abby asked, "I'm most confused about the next section of the prophecy, the whole 'golden drop thing'. There's a couple things that are bothering me about it."

"An' what would that be, Lassie?"

Abby pulled her hair behind her head as she formulated her thoughts. "Well, first off, do you think it's possible Mavis and Tavis only know about that part of the writings, seeing as how you just said you'd never heard the entire thing? It seems odd to me this was the only thing they mentioned when I was with them. Surely if they thought there was a descendant to the Red King out there, they'd be raving mad."

Agatha rubbed her chin. "It's possible, I think. When Enya scribed the scroll, rumors of its sayings traveled the countryside, but only in small bits as I already mentioned. And as those brothers can't leave this mountain, I imagine their foul thieves may 'ave run across the phrasing and told it to them. It's just a guess though."

Abby nodded. "Hmm, that might make sense. But what really doesn't make sense to me is their interpretation of 'A golden drop, the third of three, bears the power to set them free'. I mean, they must be crazy to think a girl with a golden curl that repeats some 'magic words' three times has the power to release all the faeries from Myst's spell."

"Oh, Aye," agreed Agatha with a sneer, "such foolishness to think this 'golden drop' is a curl of hair. But what I do think they 'ave right, but no' in the way they believe, is the 'third of three' is a person."

Abby thumbed her necklace and stared into the pit. "Huh. If you're right, I wonder what power the person has?"

Victoria sang with glee as Abby continued to play with her newly acquired necklace. "My sun-catcher!" Victoria scooted next to Abby and placed her hand on the smooth stone. "Did Sage give you my necklace?!"

Surprised by her mother's reaction, Abby replied, "Oh. Yes, just before I 'came' here. She said she thought you would've wanted me to have it. I hope that was okay."

Victoria clasped Abby's hands in hers. "Of course that was okay; that was very thoughtful of your sister." Victoria sighed as she stared beyond the glowing field, "I just wish the three of us could be together again."

Abby gasped and pulled her hands free. She jumped up and started pacing around the pit as the others looked on in anticipation. "The 'third of three'." Abby thumbed her mouth in thought, then continued. "This is going to sound crazy, but if Agatha is right it refers to a person, it could be my sister, Sage!! I mean, I don't know what special power she could possibly have, but what if this has something to do with a blood line, just like with the Red King." Abby looked to her mom. "You, me, and Sage...she would be the third of three, that is, if she were forced to come here and perform craziness!"

The others around the pit looked to one another with uncertainty until Agatha furthered the discussion. "Well, Lass, that isn't out of the realm of possibilities. But the question remains, if this is so, is how exactly does she fulfill the prophecy? We need to consider the final verse, it's the key, I believe. 'Fools beware, rethink yer hate, 'ere fire binds gold to seal yer fate'."

Abby continued to pace with purpose. "'Fools beware, rethink your hate'. I'm certain this is referring to Mavis and Tavis. But I have no clue what ''Ere fire binds gold' means, but whatever it is, it's going to seal their fate."

Agatha hopped up and exclaimed, "To finish Myst's

spell, to put those evil brothers where they belong once and fer all!"

At the sound of Agatha's words, cheers could be heard throughout the cave and many of the women began to gather around the fire. A new sense of confidence rushed through Abby's body as she ran to the barrier to engage Finlay. In her excitement, she yelled out, "Finlay! We think we figured out most of the prophecy. It's Sage! She's the one. I think my sister is the key!!"

Just as her final words left Abby's mouth, a thunderous clap rang through the chamber. Mavis and Tavis appeared outside the barrier, inches from where Abby stood. "Sister, eh?" said Tavis, "we'd like to meet her if you'd be so kind."

***

Horrified and shaken, Abby jumped away from the field as many of the prisoners clamored over a foot bridge into the furthest depths of the chamber. Glancing over her shoulder, she could see Agatha and her mother pushing a resistant Rory into the deepest shadows. Abby's legs quivered. She could feel Mavis's eyes tunneling into the back of her head as she slowly turned her head to face the brothers. She stammered, "Beg your pardon, Sirs, but you must have misunderstood me. There's nothing special about my sister, trust me."

Tavis seemed to grow in size as his voice boomed and green sparks jumped from his fingertips. "I have little patience today for games, my dear." Tavis turned his attention to Finlay. "What are you up to, fowl beast? You shouldn't be in here...but as you are, make use of yourself and fetch this Sister our newest guest speaks of."

Finlay's hackles rose and he let out a low, ominous growl. Mavis and Tavis looked at each other curiously, surprised by the reaction of their slave. Tavis gave a slight nod to Mavis who cackled with glee as he wrung his hands and towered over Finlay. Mavis spat at the dog. "You dare defy your Masters?" Finlay continued to growl, standing his ground. Mavis smiled as a giant green orb formed in his hand. Finlay took a step back and bared his teeth. "Very well," sung Mavis as he lobbed the sizzling ball with great force at Finlay's midsection.

Finlay howled in agony and flopped to the ground as the energy encompassed his body, crackling and popping with each twitch of his torso. As Finlay's cry diminished and he lay in silence, Abby rushed to the field and screamed out in anguish. "No! Leave him alone!" To Abby's relief, Finlay lifted his head and slowly rose. *You must remain silent, Lass. They cannot know our connection.*

Tavis scratched his chin as he turned his attention to Abby. "What's this? You have a liking for our slave?" Tavis continued to stroke a spindly finger along his jawline. "I wonder if the feeling is reciprocal?"

With desperation in her eyes, Abby remained silent as she looked from Finlay to the faeries and back.

Tavis turned to Mavis and jerked his head toward Abby. "Brother, if you would..."

Mavis grinned with pleasure and bowed. "It would be my honor, Brother." Before anyone could react, Mavis zipped through the forcefield, clamped a hand around Abby's wrist, and zipped back to stand next to his brother.

Abby cried out at the painful grip around her wrist. "Let me go, you creep!"

Mavis clucked at his struggling captive. "Tsk, tsk, where did your manners go?" As the last word left his lips, Mavis readjusted his grasp to Abby's neck. He pulled her close to him and raised his other hand to her face, placing an electrified finger to her temple. Abby gasped and held as still as she possibly could fearing Mavis might sear a hole in her head.

Finlay let out a thunderous roar that seemed to echo forever, shaking the entire chamber in its wake. When the rumbling stopped, all that could be heard throughout the cavern was the buzzing of the faerie's magic.

Tavis smiled eerily. "Well, that answers that." Positioning himself between Finlay and Abby, Tavis continued. "You will oblige our request and retrieve said Sister or watch our lovely guest here become intimately acquainted with faerie magic."

Abby willed herself not to move as Finlay began to pace in contemplation. She shifted her eyes, straining to focus through the field and into the depths of the chamber where Rory hid. She wasn't certain, but she thought she caught a glimpse of him trying to remove his disguise. Abby concentrated her focus back to Finlay and called out to him in her mind. *If you don't do what they ask, they are going to discover Rory. They will kill him, I just know it.*

Finlay snorted in response as he continued to pace. *I cannot bring another here. I will not bring another here. I refuse to be a tool in such doings anymore. It must end now, little one.*

Abby cried out desperately. *Finlay, if you don't do*

what they say, they might kill you too. I'm not excited about bringing Sage into this either, but deep down I don't believe they will actually harm any of the girls, not when they think one of us still might be the key. There's a way out of this. I feel it in my gut, we just have to get Rory to quit denying his heritage. Abby paused and let her mind relax. *Trust me, Finlay.*

Finlay snorted one last time, squared off in front of Tavis, and lowered his front torso into a bow. Tavis smiled at the submission. As Finlay rose, the air around his body crackled. In moments, the space in which he once stood was empty, save for a handful of glowing, green tendrils that fizzled into nothing. Seconds later, the air crackled again and Finlay reappeared with a dazed and disoriented Sage.

Mavis released his grasp on Abby and joined his brother. Tavis swept an arm toward Finlay and the new arrival. "There now, that wasn't so hard, was it?"

19

"Where am I?" Sage shrieked and looked frantically around the cavern, unable to comprehend what had happened to her. Not noticing Abby in her confusion, she ended her survey by locking eyes with Tavis. "Who are you?" Sage raised an eyebrow and took a step back. "What are you?"

Tavis eyed their newest captive suspiciously. Sage donned rabbit-print pajamas, fuzzy slipper socks, and a thick towel twisted atop her head. "My dear, allow me to introduce myself. My name is Tavis." Tavis proceeded to bow and swoop an arm toward Mavis. "And this, is my illustrious brother, Mavis. Please do excuse the hasty manner in which you arrived, we had little choice in the matter as your purported expertise is of immediate necessity."

Abby cleared her throat and stepped into her sister's view. Sage's jaw dropped in disbelief as she ran to Abby and hugged her tight, oblivious to the growing tension in the cave. "Abby! What on earth are you doing here? Mrs. MacTavish and I have been worried sick! We've been searching everywhere for you the last three days."

Abby glanced at the faeries uneasily as she released her arms from her sister. "Sage, there's too much to tell you and little time. What's important for you to know is those two over there," Abby jerked her head in the direction of their captors, "are going to take you somewhere else and demand you perform magic for them."

Sage snorted in response. "That's ridiculous, there's no such thing as magic."

Abby could see Mavis was becoming restless, wringing his hands with 'that look' in his eyes. Finlay circled behind the girls as Abby instructed her sister. "Sage, listen to me." Leaning in close, she whispered as silently as she could. "When they ask, say 'hocus pocus' three times...and be dramatic about it."

Sage began to tremble and jumped when she noticed the giant, green beast again. "Abby, I don't understand what's going on here. Let's just go, get out of this place."

Finlay growled in response as Tavis zipped to within inches of the sisters, green tendrils stretching from his fingertips. "I'm afraid that's not a possibility, my dear. You are our means to a long awaited end. No one is leaving."

Mavis joined his brother's side. "I'm not so sure, fine brother." Mavis gestured to the towel on Sage's head. "We cannot see if she bears the mark with that filthy rag on her head."

Tavis nodded in agreement. "So very true, Brother." Tavis stretched a pointy finger toward Sage. "If you would, please remove that garment from your head."

Unsure, Sage looked to Abby for reassurance. Abby nodded and mouthed to her sister it was okay.

Sage reached up and untwisted the damp towel. She flung her now-dry hair back and forth and let it fall freely. Her chestnut curls settled to her shoulders and her sole blond ringlet fell to frame her face.

The faeries hissed in approval. "Good, good," said Tavis, "you will come with us at once." Mavis grabbed Sage by the arm and began to whisk her out of the chamber.

Sage cried out to her sister. "Abby!"

Just as Abby was losing sight of her, she called out, "remember what I told you!"

Tavis circled Abby and her phantom. Finlay crouched into a defensive stance as Tavis spoke. "You best hope, my dear, your sister is what you say or we will most certainly have a problem. My patience wears thin." Tavis towered over Finlay. "And you, beast, I am most displeased with your behavior. However, I shall have to deal with you later, there is a more important matter at hand." Tavis began to glide from the chamber but with a flick of his hands, a new force field engulfed Abby and Finlay, trapping them where they stood. "Just to make sure you stay put, beast." And with that, Tavis was gone in a flash.

Abby slumped to the ground and whimpered as mental exhaustion took hold. Finlay had no more than burrowed his muzzle between her hands when Rory called out from behind the main barrier. "A-by! A-by! Are ye okay, A-by?"

Feeling a renewed burst of energy upon hearing Rory's voice, Abby rose to respond. "I'm okay, Rory. I'm just really worried for Sage, and, well, for all of us. It won't be long before the faeries are back with my sister and my gut tells me things are going to get real ugly then. If I'm right Sage is the key, we have to figure out the rest of the prophecy so she can put them in their place once and for all."

Rory proceeded to strip off his disguise and readjust

his own clothing. "Tell me what to do A-by an' I will do it." Rory's cheeks turned red as he pulled his sword from its makeshift scabbard for emphasis. "I will no' see ye hurt further."

Abby squinted through the two barriers unsure of what she had just witnessed. "Rory! Your sword - I think it just glowed red!"

Rory scrunched his face in surprise and held the sword aloft. Just as Abby guessed, the engravings on the blade of the sword had a faint, pulsating, red glow to them. "A-by, yer right. But I don't know why it's glowin'."

Agatha gasped and rushed to Rory's side. "Open yer mind, Laddie. Do ye remember me sayin' this sword was one of a kind? Well when the Red King yielded this sword here, he could create fire. That is how he battled the faeries."

"Fire!" Abby exclaimed. "Of course! That must be why Mavis and Tavis freaked out on those grimy thieves when I was first brought here. They were afraid of the thieves' torch!"

Rory studied his sword, his face unreadable. The glow began to fade from the engravings and Rory frowned. "It's goin' away, A-by, I don't know what to do."

Abby frantically encouraged Rory. "You must realize it's true now, Rory. You are the descendant of the Red King. You have the power within you." Abby flailed her arms for emphasis. "You have to believe in yourself, Rory."

A sense of deep contemplation washed across Rory's face as he stretched the sword in front of him and pointed the tip to the ground, examining the engravings. Abby called out to her companion one last time, not knowing what more she could say. "Rory?"

Rory looked up and met Abby's eyes. "Aye, A-by?"

"I believe in you," answered Abby with words full of truth.

Confidence swelled within Rory's eyes and in moments, the sword's blade burst into a deep, red glow that washed out the color of everything around him. Rory stood tall and a smile crept across his face. "I believe, A-by. Let the faeries return and feel the power of the Red King again!" When the last word rolled from Rory's lips, he raised the sword high and ran at the force field, letting out an emotional cry. Rory slashed at the field and when the blade connected with it, a wave of flames shot out across the entire barrier. In seconds, the main force field fizzled into nothing and the flames were sucked back into the sword's engravings. A loud cheer erupted from the chamber as the captives jumped up and down, hugging one another with joy. Rory ran across the chamber to the field surrounding Abby and Finlay. "Stand back, A-by." Abby buried herself in Finlay's thick coat as Rory swung wide from left to right at the barrier. Flames shot from the blade and ate away at the faerie magic until the only green glow left in the chamber came from Finlay, the stream, and that of the 'fire' pits.

Abby jumped up and ran to Rory, flinging her arms around him. "You did it! I knew you had it in you, Numpty!"

Finlay huffed and pawed at the ground. *Do not celebrate so quickly, Lass. The boy has not yet fulfilled that which he is destined to. My 'Masters' will return at any moment.* Finlay circled the duo and stopped with his head held high next to Rory. A phrase that Abby had pushed to the back of her mind amidst the chaos in the cavern washed through her brain. *The Red King must set me free.*

Abby smacked her forehead with her palm. "How could I have forgotten that?" Abby looked to Rory. "Rory! You have to free Finlay, quickly, before the faeries come back!"

Rory looked from his sword to Finlay to Abby. "A-by, I don't want to burn him. I'm no' sure what to do exactly."

Finlay turned his body perpendicular to the pair. *He must drive the sword through my chest.*

Abby caught her breath. "He says you have to drive the sword through his chest."

Rory frowned at the suggestion. "No, that will surely be the end of him."

Finlay stamped his front legs impatiently. *You must trust me, Lass, as I trusted in you. It is the only way for me to be truly free of the faeries' chains. Tell the boy to do it now!*

Abby choked on the words. "Rory, you must do it, now. Finlay says it's the only way, and I...I trust what he says."

Rory hesitated momentarily, then motioned for Abby to stand clear. He held the sword parallel to the ground, looked Finlay in the eye, and with a quick nod of approval, drove the sword into his chest. The cavern rumbled. Finlay shrieked in agony as an explosion of green and red enveloped him. Rory shielded his face and pulled the sword free as he backed away. Abby cried out for Finlay as good and evil battled for possession of the creature. The air crackled with electricity making the hairs on Abby's arms stand on end. Abby thought it would never stop, that she would never see her phantom again. But then something truly magical happened. The flames encapsulated Finlay until no more green tendrils were visible. And at that moment, a howl of triumph echoed throughout the chamber. As Rory's sword beckoned for its power to return home, out stepped Finlay from the inferno in his true form, that of the White Warrior.

***

He was the most magnificent thing Abby had ever seen. She wondered if Finlay were actually bigger than what she remembered, as if the faeries' magic had compressed the creature's size somehow. His fur was whiter than fresh fallen snow and flowed in such a manner that she could feel its warmth just by gazing upon him. Not a soul in the chamber let a breath slip as Finlay shook his body fervently from head to toe and stepped forward to bow before Rory. Finlay caressed Abby's mind. *Tell the boy I am forever in his debt.*

Abby ran to Finlay and wrapped her arms around his neck. She looked to Rory and relayed the dog's gratitude, then buried herself in the warrior's luxurious coat. "Oh Finlay," she cried, "I'm so glad you're okay, I thought you were gone."

Finlay pawed the ground. *If it is in my power, little one, I will never leave you. But we must make haste. We have yet to discover the true key to stopping this insanity.*

Abby ran her hands through Finlay's fur one last time and stood straight. "You're right." Abby turned to Rory and motioned for her mother and Agatha to join them. "We have to decipher the end of the prophecy, and quick, I fear we are running out of time. Now, we have already guessed the 'third of three' line must refer to a person. My gut says it's my sister, but we still don't know what the 'golden drop' is."

Agatha nodded. "Aye, an' the part about 'fire binding gold', me thinks it's the most important part of all!"

"Fire!" Abby smiled and jumped excitedly. "Fire. Rory's sword! There must be a connection there." Abby began to pace. "Rory's sword must bind with something gold." Scratching her head, Abby continued. "I bet it's the same gold as this 'golden drop', if we could just figure out..." Before Abby could finish her thought, a thunderous howl blasted through the chamber. Abby gulped as Mavis, Tavis, and a visibly disturbed Sage appeared in the middle of the chamber.

The brothers stared in disbelief at the lack of force fields and began quarreling with one another at how such as thing could have happened. Sage took advantage of the moment and ran to Abby. Abby hugged her sister quickly, knowing Sage had no clue about their mom. Abby kept her voice low and beckoned for Sage to follow her to where their mom and Agatha had retreated. "Sage, don't freak out on me," Abby gestured to their mom, "but there's someone here I'd like you to 'meet'." Sage stared in utter disbelief as their mother hugged her, after which, she promptly fainted. Abby rolled her eyes. *Figures.* Victoria and Agatha pulled Sage to the chamber wall, propping her up and fanning her face.

While the family reunion transpired, Tavis realized his

most recent captive was no longer in his vicinity. He spun around to find her and met the gaze of Finlay, massive and powerful, and no longer his slave. Finlay leaped forward in front of Abby and landed with a defensive posture. Tavis roared at the sight as he grabbed Mavis to confirm what he was seeing. Mavis turned and let out a shriek like that of no other. It was of such force, those closest to its source stumbled backward to regain their balance. It was not Finlay that Mavis locked eyes with, but Rory, who stood tall and solid with his sword ready. "It cannot be so, Brother," screeched Mavis, "we killed that foul creature ourselves! And that sword!! How is it he has that sword?"

Rory yelled out to the faeries as they approached him with green orbs in hand. "I am Rory McKay from the Clan McKay, just and true descendant of the Red King, and I am here to stop ye."

Tavis came to an abrupt halt, followed by Mavis, just yards from Rory. "Is that so?" Tavis sneered at his adversary. "We shall see, fool. We put you in the ground once and will take great pleasure in doing it again. May you haunt us no more!" The faeries raised their hands in front of them and flung multiple orbs in succession at Rory. Rory dodged from side to side, then swung his sword with an unnatural precision. Flames connected with those orbs that didn't fly over Rory's head. In mere seconds, the orbs were swallowed up by the fire. The faeries cursed and spat as they readied for another assault.

Rory and the faeries continued to battle, orbs and flames flying every which way. For fear any number of the captives might get hurt, Abby called out to Finlay. *You* must get as many of those girls to safety as you can! Is it possible for you to take them back to their rightful times and homes?

Finlay huffed and pawed at the ground. *Aye, Lass, I could do that, but I am hesitant to leave you.*

Abby sighed. *I understand, but I'll be okay. These people have been through enough, I don't want to see them injured. You must seize the opportunity to make things right. Now! Please, Finlay!*

Finlay was silent for a moment but soon swayed his head in agreement. *It will be then. You must communicate to them what I am about to do.*

Abby was off in a flash before Finlay finished the thought. She ducked low and ran the span of the chamber as fast as she could, leaping over the stream without hesitation. She motioned wildly for everyone to gather with her. Her explanation to the captives of what was about to happen was met with great joy and relief. "Finlay is going to take each of you home one at a time. All you have to do is put your hand on his head when he approaches you. I guess you'll have to tell him where to go, but I don't know how you decide about 'when'. I know some of you have been gone a very long time." Abby smiled at everyone around her. "It's all going to be okay."

Abby called out to Finlay that it was safe to proceed. The group jumped when Finlay's massive form appeared unexpectedly feet away. Abby ran to her warrior and hugged him. *I've got to tell Mom, Sage, and Agatha what's happening. I'll see you soon.*

Abby could feel concern and a hint of fear when Finlay responded. *Aye, child. Be careful.*

20

*R*ory continued to fight the brothers with fervor as Abby repeated the process of jumping the stream and crouching low as she dashed to the other side of the chamber. She glanced over her shoulder to see Elli place a hand on Finlay's head. With a brilliant flash of white light, the two were gone. Abby turned her attention to her mom, sister, and Agatha, who were now huddled under a small overhang of the chamber wall, seeking refuge from stray magic flung haphazardly. Sage seemed to have her senses about her again as she exchanged words with Victoria.

Abby crouched low next to her elders. "Finlay is taking as many people home as he can. It's up to us to figure out the rest of the prophecy. I don't know how much longer Rory can continue. It looks like he's getting tired." Abby cried out as an orb, followed by a streak of flames, zipped within inches of her chest. Sage pulled her sister back against the wall. "Abby! Are you okay?"

Abby's hoodie was singed, so she unzipped the jacket to check her torso for burns. "Yeah, I think so. That was a little too close for my liking though." Just as Abby relaxed, another stray flame shot past the huddling group. This time, however, a portion of the flame snaked its way back to Abby and flicked the surface of her amulet before withdrawing back to Rory's sword.

Sage stared at Abby's sternum with an odd look on her face. "Um, Abby?"

Abby returned the odd look. "What is it, Sage?"

Sage pointed to Abby's chest. "The necklace is glowing!"

Abby scrunched her face and held the amulet up in her hand. "Whoa..."

All eyes in the little group focused on the stone in Abby's hand. Agatha extended a finger toward the stone. "Has it ever done that before, Lassie?"

Abby contemplated the question and looked to her sister who promptly shrugged. Abby shook her head. "Not that I know of. What about you, Mom? Did you ever see the stone glow?"

Victoria considered the question carefully, "I don't believe so, Abigail."

Abby stared intently at the stone. She thought she could see something red inside of it. "Hey. It looks like there's a faint symbol in the middle of it now!"

Agatha leaned in close to focus her aged eyes. "Aye, Abby, indeed there is."

Abby eyed the symbol suspiciously. *That sure looks familiar.* Abby looked to Victoria. "Mom, where exactly did you get this necklace?"

Victoria smiled as she searched her memories. "Dear, Mrs. MacTavish gave it to me. And if I recall correctly, she said it had been passed down in her family from mother to daughter, over and over. For centuries, I think. She gave it to me because she never had any children of her own, and well, she said I was like kin to her."

Agatha gasped, startling the others. "No...it can't be!"

A mixture of excitement and confusion washed across Abby's face. "What can't be, Agatha?"

"Well, Lassie, I once heard before Sylvan Myst died, he bestowed a magical amulet to his daughter, Enya. It was said to equal the power of the Red King." Agatha cupped Abby's hand underneath and raised the necklace level with her eyes. "Me thinks this is the 'golden drop' of the prophecy."

Sage questioned with a raised eyebrow. "Not that I know who these people are, but just say this really is the amulet of Enya. Does that mean Mrs. MacTavish is an ancestor of this Sylvan Myst? And what exactly are we supposed to do with it?"

Abby tilted the necklace and looked straight down at the pulsing symbol inside. A flip switched in her brain as she recognized the shape of the symbol. Her eyes shot up to find Rory and the sword he wielded. *Fire binds gold.* Abby excitedly brought her attention back to the group. "The hilt of the sword...I...I think the stone fits in it!"

Victoria encouraged her youngest. "Abigail, can you recite the prophecy to us once more?"

Abby nodded, knowing it would be forever engraved in her memory.

> Green tendrils reign
> Engulf the land
> A rightful warrior
> Will come again.
> Heart and hand
> Head of fire

A just, true soul
Regains the power.
A golden drop
The third of three
Bears the power
To set them free.
Fools beware
Rethink your hate
'Ere fire binds gold
To seal your fate.

Chills ran down her spine as Abby looked to her sister. "Sage. It's up to you. You're the one. You have to place it in the sword."

Sage cringed at the faeries' screams. Trembling, she outstretched the palm of her hand to take the necklace from her sister. Abby removed the amulet from its chain and handed it to Sage. The stone suddenly lost its glow and the inner symbol faded. Sage frowned. "What happened to it?"

Abby wrinkled her brow. "Hmm. That's odd." Abby stretched her hand out to examine the stone. As soon as Abby's fingers touched the smooth surface, the glow returned. Perplexed, Abby placed the amulet back into Sage's hand where it promptly dimmed to nothing. Abby scratched her forehead. "This doesn't make any sense." Abby looked to Victoria. "Mom, try picking up the stone and see what happens."

Victoria acknowledged her daughter's request and promptly took the amulet in her hand. There was no change in the appearance of the stone. Victoria stretched her hands out, cupped Abby's in her own, and released the amulet to her daughter. The stone pulsed again in Abby's hands. "Abigail, my sweet, do you not see what's happening here?" Abby met her mother's eyes. "Sage is not the one as told in the prophecy. You are the 'third of three'. It was not the order we were brought here that was the key. You are the third in our bloodline, you are the key. It's up to you to save us all." Victoria stroked Abby's cheek as she continued. "Just as the prophecy says, you 'bear the power to set them free'...to set us free."

Missiles of magic and fire continued to fly recklessly throughout the cavern. The sound of Rory's cries and grunts brought Abby back from her moment of deep contemplation, understanding, and acceptance. Abby squeezed the amulet tight in her palm and lifted her head to the eyes awaiting her. Abby's body trembled. *Why was I so blind! It's been me all along. And the answer has been hanging around my neck the entire time!* Abby stuffed her frustration down deep and looked from one person to the next. Letting out a deep breath, she confidently said, "Okay. I can do this! But, I think I'm going to need some help. I'm not sure how I can get anywhere near Rory, let alone the hilt of his sword."

"You need a distraction," said Sage.

Agatha nodded. "Aye, a distraction." Agatha scanned the chamber, considering its contents. "Hmm, I 'ave an idea. Victoria, would ye come with me please?"

Victoria nodded and squeezed her daughters' hands. "What do you have in mind, my friend?"

Agatha motioned for Victoria to follow her. "Ye shall see. It's simple but may give Abby the time she needs." Agatha turned to Abby and gave her an assuring smile.

"Act fast, Lassie, when the moment comes."

Abby nodded. "I will, I promise. But, what are you going to do?"

Agatha chuckled again with a sly grin and added. "I'm goin' to introduce those devils to a little friend of mine."

As Agatha and her mother started picking their way across the cavern, Abby turned her attention to the other captives, wondering if Finlay was successful in taking them home. Her warrior was nowhere to be seen, but she could just make out four or five women crouched low awaiting their turn for freedom. As Abby looked on, Sage gently grabbed her shoulders and turned her sister toward her. "Abby, I want you to know something."

"What is it, Sage."

"I still don't completely understand what's going on here, and Mom... geez, I can't wrap my brain around it. But, no matter what happens, I want you to know I'm really proud of you."

Abby hugged her sister. "Thanks, Sage. That means a lot coming from you. But don't worry, we're going to get out of here."

Sage released her arms and gave Abby's hand a reassuring squeeze. "I have faith in you, little sister." Sage gave Abby a devilish grin and added, "And your friend over there," Sage continued with a wink, "it looks like you found yourself a nice, Scottish lad."

Abby groaned and turned her attention to Agatha and their mother. The women each had something in hand and were slowly sneaking along the perimeter of the cave toward the ongoing battle. They stepped across the stream at its narrowest point and kept low to the shadows. The faeries were so driven by their rage toward the Red King, they were oblivious to all other actions in the chamber. Abby squinted in effort to determine what the women were carrying. *Are those pots?* Abby giggled to herself. *Well, it worked for me and Rory's mom!* Agatha and Victoria crouched down and positioned themselves behind Mavis and Tavis. They appeared to be in silent discussion about the best plan of attack. Abby rolled the amulet in her hand and whispered the prophecy to herself as the moments ticked by. Sage nudged Abby in the side. "Abby, can you tell what Mom and Agatha are doing?"

Abby replied quietly without taking her eyes from the clash. "I think they want to hit the faeries on their heads with a couple of pots, but it seems they are having a disagreement about the best time to do it."

Before Abby knew what was happening, Sage sighed, mumbled to herself and sprinted toward the center of the chamber. "I hope I won't regret this!" As she reached the middle of the cave, Sage jumped up and down, waving her arms wildly, and yelled as loud as she could at her captors. "Hey you! Over here! I figured out how to free your 'brethren'." To Sage's amazement, Mavis, Tavis, and Rory paused mid-strike and looked with surprise to the source of exclamation.

As Sage hoped, Agatha and Victoria made good of the pause in battle. The women closed the distance between themselves and the faeries as fast as they could and raised their pots in unison. A loud whack rang out as Agatha and Victoria made contact with their targets. The faeries groaned, stumbling as they each grabbed the back of their head. Abby focused on the sword as she began to rise, unaware of the presence now next to her. *Place your hand upon my head, child, and we shall end this together.*

A warm rush of happiness flooded Abby's body upon Finlay's sudden appearance. She confidently placed her hand upon his head and welcomed the strange sensation of spontaneous travel. Moments later, Abby and the white warrior stood next to Rory. Agatha and Victoria continued to crack the faeries over the head, giving Abby the time she needed. "Rory! Hold out your sword so I can see the hilt."

Rory appeared confused by the request but did as he was asked. Sweat rolled from his forehead and he welcomed the moment of rest. "What's happenin' A-by? Did ye discover somethin'?"

Abby held the stone out for Rory to see. "Rory, what was it you told me Sylvan Myst said to his daughter on his death bed?"

Curious about the question, Rory replied without pause. "With light comes freedom. Why do ye ask, A-by?"

Abby glanced over her shoulder to see Agatha, Victoria, and Finlay pinning the faeries to the ground. She looked back to Rory and held the stone up between two fingers. The glow from Rory's sword enhanced the beating color of the gem. The symbol inside the stone blazed a deep red. "This is the solution, Rory, and I've had it all along! This is the power Sylvan bestowed to Enya. The power that is going to stop this craziness."

Abby looked to the hilt of the sword and pointed excitedly. "Rory! Look!" The section of the hilt in which Abby suspected the stone would fit burned a bright yellow and began to pulsate in unison with the stone, beckoning it to its rightful place. Abby sucked in a deep breath and worked the stone into the indentation in the sword's hilt. As she did, she released her breath and whispered, "With light comes freedom." When the stone was firmly snapped in place, a blinding blast of yellow light filled the entire chamber. A roar emanated from the sword and Abby felt as if she couldn't breathe. Mavis and Tavis shrieked and clawed at the ground. Their bodies began to move upward against their will, out of the twisted pile of arms, legs, and pots. It was as if a giant, invisible vacuum were sucking the faeries into the air.

Abby tried to scream over the rumbling in the chamber. "Rory? What's happening?"

Rory motioned with his hands he couldn't hear Abby's question as Mavis grabbed for one of his braids. Rory ducked to avoid the faerie's grasp and watched in disbelief as the brothers continued to rise up in the air, feet first, arms flailing.

The blinding light, the roar, and the screams from the faeries seemed to go on forever. Abby wondered how this would end, and then she had her answer. As the light faded and the roar diminished, Mavis and Tavis were sucked into the ceiling of the chamber. When all was silent, two sets of eyes, forever embedded, glared down upon the small group.

21

*A*gatha was first to break the eerie silence. "Well now," she said with a smirk, "seems to be a fittin' place for those two."

Sage ran to the group and helped her mother and Agatha to their feet. "Is everyone okay?"

Abby stared at the ceiling in disbelief and questioned to no one in particular. "Is it really over?"

Rory grunted in agreement to the query as his muscles quivered from exhaustion.

Abby felt a cold nose burrow into the palm of her hand. *Aye child, you have fulfilled the prophecy.*

Abby smiled and ran her fingers through Finlay's fur. *Finlay?*

Yes, Lass?

Abby looked quizzically at the dog. *Did you know all along I'd be the one to lock the faeries up?*

Finlay swayed his head. *This, I did not know.*

Abby broadcast a thought before Finlay could continue. *Well, there's something I haven't been able to figure out.*

Finlay nudged Abby with his nose. *Go on.*

The night when you first appeared to Sage and I...you intended to bring her here, didn't you?

E M McIntyre

Aye, Lass, that I did.

Abby furrowed her brow. *So why didn't you take her then, or me, for that matter? I thought once you'd made a connection with someone, the faerie magic would pull you back?*

Finlay snorted a blast of hot air into Abby's hand. *It's true, Lass, but only if they had sent me out specifically to search for a 'key'. And as you have learned, I must touch the person for my abilities to work. When you caused the transport you were in to make that blaring noise, it broke my pull to your sister.*

Abby snorted. *Oh, you mean when I honked the horn it distracted you?*

Aye, Lass, as you say.

So why didn't you suck me back in time right then and there?

Finlay pawed at the ground. *When you pulled my attention from your sister, I knew instantly we had a special connection. And when I first entered your mind, I sensed you were courageous and clever enough to face an uncertain adventure. I knew if I planted the seed of mystery in your mind, you would find the hidden scroll. It was fortunate when I happened upon you the second time - I had been released to hunt for dear. It wasn't until then I could bring you to this time and place.*

Abby rubbed her back at the memory. *And drop me smack on top of Rory.*

Finlay bowed his head. *Aye, Lass. My apologies for the miscalculation.*

Abby smiled, wrapped her arms around her warrior's deep chest, and sunk her face into his lush fur. *That's okay, fur-ball, I forgive you. I don't know that I believe in fate, but it sure seems like things worked out the way they were meant to.*

Growing uneasy in the emptiness of the cave, Sage cleared her throat to gain everyone's attention. "Abby, not to interrupt your cuddle time, but can we please get out of here? This place is giving me the creeps."

Abby stood and looked around the cave. A quick head count came to five, plus one magical dog. *Good, Finlay took everyone else home.*

Victoria beamed at her daughters. "Sage is right. It's time for all of us to finally go home. Your father will certainly be surprised to see me."

Abby frowned, hoping she wouldn't disappoint her mother. "Mom, don't be sad, but Dad is off searching for a special book. I doubt he's home."

Sage looked to their mother. "Abby's right, Mom. He's not back yet."

Victoria rubbed Abby's shoulder. "No worries, my sweet. We will all be together again soon enough. At least we have a cherished friend awaiting us at the bookstore."

Abby burst into giggles at the sudden thought. "Oh Mom, I can't wait to see the look on Mrs. MacTavish's face when you show up! She is not going to believe this!"

Victoria smiled as she imagined the moment but then began to frown as she turned to Agatha. "My dear friend," said Victoria, taking Agatha's hand, "I'm going to miss our long talks." Victoria gave a gentle squeeze to the woman's hand. "And it's truly a shame you will never meet Mrs. MacTavish. I'm certain you would have gotten on well with one another. You remind me so much of her."

Agatha squished Victoria's hand in return, then pulled it away to rest it on a hip. "Well. Now there's an interestin' idea! What's to say I can't come with ye? I would much fancy meetin' another descendant of Myst." Agatha noted Victoria's look of surprise and continued with a touch of excitement in her voice. "An', I must say, me friend, listenin' to all yer stories of where ye come from...would be quite an adventure for an old lady."

Rory took Abby's hand before anyone could reply. "I too want to go with ye, A-by. There's nothin' left for me here. An' if this Mrs. MacTavish is really me kin, I want to meet her." Rory looked down at the ground and appeared to blush. "An' I'm no' ready to say farewell to ye, A-by."

Abby's cheeks grew red as she looked to her mom for guidance. "I...I'm not so sure that's such a smart idea, for either of you to come back with us. I mean, things are a lot different than what you know here. What do you think, Mom?"

As Victoria started to reply, Finlay let out a rumble that silenced the cavern and drew all eyes to him. He circled the group slowly and then stopped to lean against Abby. *Do not be so quick to dismiss the requests. Your paths are intertwined more than you realize.*

Abby raised an eyebrow. *And you know that how, exactly?*

Finlay seemed reluctant to reply as he pawed at the ground. *I have seen it, Lass.*

What? You mean you've been even further into the future than when you 'took' me?

Aye, child. We will have more mysteries to solve.

Abby balled her fists and placed them on her hips.

What mysteries? Pausing, Abby took a step back. *Wait. You said 'we'. Does that mean you're coming with us?*

Finlay snorted and bowed his head. *I cannot say more, but yes, I am coming with you if you will have me.*

Abby lurched forward and wrapped her arms around Finlay's neck. *Of course I want you to come with me! I can't imagine a day without you.*

Abby looked up to the group's expecting eyes. "Well, it's settled. Finlay says we are all to go home together." Abby looked to her mom. "I can keep him, can't I?"

Victoria watched as Abby smothered her face in the beast's thick coat. "Of course you may, Abigail. It seems to me he was a victim in all of this too, I'd say he needs a good home now."

Abby giggled with happiness. "Thanks, Mom." Winking at Finlay, Abby added, "I promise I won't let him cause too much trouble."

Sage looked to Victoria with an air of impatience. "Mom? Would you please tell my sister to have her dog take us home now?"

Abby rolled her eyes in response. "Alright, alright." Abby motioned for everyone to gather close. "Listen up, everyone. Let's all link hands and then I'll place one of mine on Finlay's head. I'm sure everyone remembers what happens after that, to some extent."

The others nodded in agreement and grabbed a hand.

Abby slid her fingers in between Rory's. "Are you sure you're ready for this, Numpty? Some things are probably going to be scary to you." Abby paused and made a funny face. "You don't need to worry though, I'll protect you."

Rory squeezed Abby's hand and returned the funny

face with a smile. "I 'ave no doubt."

Pleased everyone seemed ready for their journey, Abby turned to Finlay. *Okay, my white warrior, take us home.*

Finlay bowed low and then raised his head next to Abby's free hand. *Whenever you are ready, my little one.*

Abby smiled, took a deep breath, and sunk her fingers into the fur on Finlay's head.

A flash of brilliant, white light engulfed the group, momentarily taking their breaths away. And then everything went black.

To my readers, I am sincerely grateful
that you have joined me on this journey.
It has been a goal long anticipated
to create a world for others to step into.
I hope you enjoyed Abby's adventure thus far;
there is more to come.
If you liked (or disliked)
The Phantom of Faerie Mountain,
I would be humbled if you left a review
at your favorite online retailer.

I would like to take a moment
to acknowledge my late mother, Vicki M McIntyre.
Her love, guidance, support, and wicked-smart intellect
helped make this story what it is.
I would not be writing this
without all of herself that she graciously gave to me.
I miss our weekend phone calls, Momma.

Visit me at:
redkingtrilogy.com
or
www.facebook.com/TheRedKingTrilogy

The Secret of Berry Brae Circle

Book 2

The Red King Trilogy

1

*A*bby opened her eyes. A blinding white mist engulfed her. She could see nothing through the haze. She squinted, her eyelids fluttering until she grew accustomed to the light. A hollow feeling inside gnawed at her gut—something wasn't right. *Where am I? Where are the others?* Abby panicked when she realized her companions were no longer present. It seemed only minutes ago Finlay used his special powers to teleport the group from deep inside the mountain. *What if those creepy faerie brothers escaped and captured them again? Please let this be a dream.* She called out into the oppressive barrier, "Mom? Sage?" Whirling her head around, she continued, "Rory? Finlay? Agatha?" After several moments of quiet, she called for Finlay with her mind. *Finlay? Can you hear me? Where are you?* When no answer came, she wanted to run, to break free from the mist. *I have to find them!* She broke into a sprint but realized she wasn't moving. Sensing no solid surface beneath her, Abby looked down into the mist and searched with her fingers. *What the...where are my feet?* Her heart raced. *Where are my legs?* Abby straightened and brought her hands in front of her face. She sighed with relief upon seeing them. *I'm not going crazy, I'm just disoriented by this stupid mist.* Abby stretched low again to verify her feet were there. When she felt nothing for the second time, she gasped, straightened up, and reached for her face. Again, her fingertips felt no sensation. *This isn't possible. I must be dreaming.* Placing her hands in front of her face again, Abby attempted to calm herself. *Get a grip, Abby. Freaking out won't help anything.* She held her hands still while watching the mist swirl. Abby drew a sharp breath as the haze curled around, and then through, her fingers. *No way. I, I'm invisible or something? What the heck is happening?* As she stood bewildered, a distant, ethereal voice called out to her. Abby craned her neck and listened, hoping the faint sound wasn't her imagination. An eternity passed before the voice repeated itself. "Amaray, find your way home."

Who's Amaray? Battling her confusion, Abby called out. "Hello? Who's there?"

"Amaray, all will be lost without you..." The wispy voice trailed off into the distance one last time.

Abby contemplated the strange words. *Sure seemed like she was talking to me. Hate to disappoint though; no Amaray here. At least, not that I can see.* Abby snorted. *Speaking of seeing, what's the deal with this mist? I'd like to know where I am so I can get out of here.*

As Abby further inspected her surroundings, a familiar, rough accent made its way to her ear. "A-by?"

Her heart skipped a beat. *Is that Rory?* His voice beckoned to her again. Abby was certain he was not far.

"Rory!" She called out with fervor. "Rory. Where are you? Can you see me?" She spun around in search of her companion, her Red King. Because he now believed in the power coursing through his blood, confidence welled within Abby. He could help her find a way out of this void.

Rory called to her again. This time Abby swore he was standing right next to her. "A-by. A-by. Wake up."

Abby paused. *I knew it. I'm dreaming. But this mist looks so real. And that woman's voice.* As Abby called out again, she felt an unusual tugging from inside her belly button. The sensation strengthened, turning into a pinch. "Ouch!" Abby reached for her stomach, still surprised when her hand passed through her midsection.

"A-by. Come back to us." Rory's voice was full of emotion.

"Rory, I'm..." The tugging ended with a final, harsh pull that swept Abby from her feet. A wave of blackness washed over her as the misty prison disappeared.

Available at your favorite online retailer!

About The Author

E M McIntyre is the author of the Red King Trilogy. Her first novel, The Phantom of Faerie Mountain won 1st place in YA Fiction for the 2016 Purple Dragonfly awards and Silver placement for YA Mystery in the 2016 Readers' Favorite awards. E M is a member of the Society of Children's Book Writers and Illustrators. She lives in Nebraska where she works as a Pediatric Cancer research lab manager. When not daydreaming of magic, mystery, and mischievous characters, E M enjoys gardening and spending time with her crazy pack of Italian greyhounds.

CPSIA information can be obtained
at www.ICGtesting.com
Printed in the USA
LVOW11s0210250517
535500LV00055B/308/P